Haidji

Harables

Short Stories 2

Haidji

This book is dedicated to Allegra

Haidji

Harables

Table of Contents

Haidji

"No matter which way you take in your life, you will arrive at your Final Destination"

Haidji – Final Destination

Haidji

Final Destination

After several rainy days, the sun decided to shine over the city.

From his bed, switching the alarm off for the third or fourth time, all that Mark could see was that there were no rain drops sliding down his windows.

Even living on the twentieth floor in one of several skyscrapers in the city did not enable him to have the sun shining into his bedroom. The next building was too close. No space for sunrays. Only light filtered by skyscrapers' morning shadows. No wonder that it was not easy to wake up. There was never really sunlight inside.

"No rain drops today, can it be that it is sunny outside?" said Mark to himself, going out of his bed.

"Why does the elevator take so long to come, every time I'm late?" murmured Mark, pressing the elevator's call button again and again, as would a mysterious law of physics make it come faster if you push the button again...and again...and again. Like parents who seem to believe that their teenage kids will go out of their beds faster in the morning if they call them several times, Mark kept pressing the button.

It neither works with teenagers, nor with elevators.

But maybe to try...makes you feel that you are doing something to rush things. And when it finally happens, because it's time for it, or because time passed by (in the elevator case), or they go finally go out of bed by their own will (in the teenagers' case), it makes you feel good that you did something for it.
But the truth is, that it does not help or work at all.

Eager to feel the sun on his face during the few steps to his workplace, it wasn't easy for Mark to wait.
"Maybe I should take the stairs today," thought Mark, while he imagined himself running all the way down to the street. He wanted to arrive earlier at work; it was his first "own office" and even having only two employees, it took him years to come to the position of being a Boss, and he wanted to be a good one.

More people came to wait in front of the elevator.

Haidji

Beatrice, who lived in the apartment across from his, came too.

Beatrice was a harp player in the Vancouver Symphony Orchestra. A graduate of the University of Toronto's Bachelor of Music program, she already performed works written for her. Her presence was intimidating for Mark. He never know what to say to her; every time he tried to impress her, he said the wrong thing, as would his words decide to be the most tuneless thing she would ever hear. Yes, he had a crush on her.

Even so, they used to stop at Starbucks and drink a coffee together before work. Walking mostly in silence. Beatrice had a crush on Mark too.

"Coffee today, Mark?" asked Beatrice.

"Sure," answered Mark. "I think I will take the stairs, go to Starbucks and wait for you in front of the building. The elevator is taking years to come. See you soon, Beatrice."

"But..."

Mark disappeared before Beatrice could say something.

The stairs.

It was slippery.

Cleaning service in the early morning.

Yellow plastic signs on the floor.

"Wet Floor" between the 20th and the 19th floors.

Between the 18th and the 17th floors, someone decided to leave an old chair.

Between the 12th and the 11th, there were someone's garbage bags.

Even with the feeling that he was running, it was taking very long for Mark to go the way he had chosen.

On the 6th floor there was a group of teenagers who decided to skip school, sitting on the steps, hanging out, deciding if they would go outside or just stay there until lunch time.
Small talk.
"No school today, guys?"
"Not really," said one of the teenagers.
"Not since we missed it," said another one.
"It is not your business," completed a third one.
"Be polite, Andrea Bonicelli... We are all sick," said a girl, who laughed.
"School on sunny days makes us sick, you know...?" said Andrea Bonicelli, trying to be polite.

Mark laughed and continued his way down.

On the 4th floor there was a white cat. Lost.
Mark had seen a few days ago a notice on the entrance board, about a lost white cat. The cat was very thin; it could have been living on the stairs for days.
Mark took the cat in his arms and continued to go down the steps.

His suit was full with cat hair, not the best example for his new employees, but he could not leave the cat there.

On the second floor, there was a Homeless person sleeping on the steps. No one knows how he managed to pass by the building's Doorman. There were so many Homeless people in the city, sleeping on the streets, in shop entrances and everywhere where they could find a free spot. Like living sleeping sculptures, made by a poor god's artist with no money to put them in a gallery.

Mark needed to balance his hands on the walls, and step carefully, to not wake him up. He stopped, holding the cat with one hand to reach for his wallet, and left some dollars for the sleeping old man.

Mark arrived on the ground floor.

He gave the cat to the Doorman and was out of the building.

"Now…to Starbucks!"

Turning right towards the closest Starbucks, Mark already started to walk as he could hear someone calling for him.

"Mark!"

It was Beatrice, and she was holding two coffee cups.

"Mark! I went to Starbucks to see if you were still there and decided to bring the coffee for you. Where were you? Running a marathon?"

"Kind of."

"Take the elevator next time, Mark... it is faster."

"I'll think about it. Actually it was... challenging."

"Challenging?" asked Beatrice.

On the way to the office, drinking his coffee, walking through the street with Beatrice, Mark told her about his journey through the stairs, and did not feel tuneless. It was as would he have made a trip to a completely different world.

Beatrice invited Mark to see her next concert.

His opening up to her gave her the courage to do so.

There were more coffee days and there was no more silence between them.

It is not always easy to decide between taking the elevator, or the stairs, in life. No matter which way you take in your life, you will arrive at your final destination. But you can choose the way you take.

Between the peace of waiting for the elevator and the adventure of taking the stairs, what do you prefer?

Haidji

"To not create expectations doesn't kill your dreams."

Haidji – The Dress

Haidji

The Dress

The finest ivory mulberry silk, made by a process the Chinese developed thousands of years ago.
The most beautiful gold lace...Venetian gold lace, of course.
People dancing in a masquerade ball staring at her, as would their eyes be speaking to her...
Mulberry silk, Venetian gold lace...Mulberry silk, Venetian gold lace...Mulberry silk, Venetian gold lace...
Venetian gold lace...silk...Venetian gold lace...
Andrea Bettencourt woke up.

The Dress!!! She knew how to make it.
Drinking her first morning coffee made with her new Red Bialetti Moka.
Italian coffee, of course, one of the few treasures in her daily life. Feeling the sun shining from outside, Andrea started to work on her newest idea.

The night and the stars inspired her creation, a dress that being inspired by the night, should not be blue and black, but white and gold.
Gold like the stars and white like the light of dreams, while the blue of the sky and the darkness of the night makes us dream about things.

She had the lace already. From her last trip to Venice, her best friend Samantha brought her some gold lace.

"Mulberry silk, where to find it?" thought Andrea as she was searching for it online.

"It is very expensive!"

Andrea used all her savings to buy white Mulberry silk.

With a Savings-less bank account, inside of a food-less atelier, she started to work on her newest project.

It wasn't that she couldn't afford much of anything; it was that she couldn't afford anything but to work on her dreams.

A few days later Samantha stopped by and brought her some fruits and sandwiches.

"Hi, starving artist, how is it going?"

"I think it is great! This is the best idea I ever had. Would you like to see it tomorrow? I want to work more on it before showing it to you."

"Of course! I'm sure it looks fantastic!"

Andrea's atelier was small and had only one vitrine that she used to expose her newest creation.

The last dress was sold awhile ago and the space was empty, decorated with drawings of her old and new ideas and some lose pieces like a blouse and a skirt hanging on a wire, as would they be drying, things she made once, years ago.

Samantha was her friend. Her best friend. The one that believed in her ideas. The one that could cheer her up when she was down.

The one that was always there for her. The one she was always there for too, hearing about her stressful work being a businesswoman in a male world.

They could spend all night speaking, if they wouldn't be both so busy working and needy for sleep hours.

"Come back tomorrow and I can show it to you," said Andrea.

"Good, I will let you work now.

If you need something, just tell."

"Bye."

"Bye."

The Dress was a materialized dream.

Even being white it remembered the blue of the night.

The Venetian gold lace reminded of thousands of stars.

Andrea made it twice. Twice, the same size. She had just enough material for that.

Exhausted after a week working almost all the time, an un-endless week, without such things called weekends.

Andrea placed her almost-ready newest creation on the vitrine and took the drawings, blouse and the skirt out of there. They were her emergency things for when the vitrine was empty.

Samantha came by as she was doing it.

"Wow! It looks great! Amazing!"

"Yes, it is almost ready, but I wanted to see how it looks."

"Will you go to the Ceremony?" Samantha asked.

Yes, it was this design prize ceremony, one of the kinds they used to go to together.

"Me? No, the invitation is too expensive for me. It is too expensive...

I don't have money for it," said Andrea.

"Oh, that's sad. I will go there. All I need is a new dress for it."

"I made two of these. I can give you one, if you like, I think it is your size."

Samantha tried the dress; it was almost perfect for her. With some small details to finish, Andrea spent the night working on it and it was ready for Samantha to pick up in the next morning.

To not create expectations doesn't kill your dreams.

They are always there, deep inside of you. To not have expectations neither avoids you to feel sad when they don't happen, nor makes you stop to believe that they can.

Andrea did not expect Samantha to invite her to go with her, but somewhere inside she dreamed about it. They always used to go to these design prize ceremonies together. It was part of their time together out of work and workspace. The real price of the dress was 10 times more expensive than an invitation to this ceremony could be. She worked 40 hours on it. Samantha could have invited her, if she wanted to.

The dress was ready in the morning. Andrea offered the dress to Samantha. She wanted her friend to look beautiful at the ceremony.

Samantha could have invited Andrea, but she did not. She thought that she already helped a lot, she was the one that gave her the Venetian gold lace anyway, and it was time for Andrea to wake up. In Samantha's mind it was time for Andrea to deserve to be invited for things. What would only happen when she would have more zeros on the right side of her bank account balance. The right side instead of the left one.

After working on it all morning long, Andrea hung the second dress on the vitrine. For sale. Kind of sad for making great dresses for a ceremony she could not go to. But, life is like it is.

Isn't it?

Miranda was walking on the street on the way to the ceremony.

She was the organizer and she still did not have a dress.

Rushing to work, speaking on the phone, she took the wrong street and was suddenly in a side street, stopped in front of a small vitrine, looking at a dress.

"Is it white and gold or blue and black?"

It was white and gold but it reminded her of a starry night.

"Wow, what a dress!"

Miranda entered the place, where Andrea was now drinking her probably third coffee of the day. Trying to focus on her work instead of thinking about friends and design ceremonies.

"Did you make that dress?" asked Miranda as she entered the place.

"Yes."

"I want to buy it. I need it now! It is fantastic! Amazing!

Samantha was at the prize ceremony with another friend.

Her phone was ringing inside of her purse but she was too busy to take the call.

With her was Carl, a good friend who made compliments about the dress she was wearing.

"It looks great, but I think it would look even greater with this red band around your waist," and he handed her a synthetic red band that Samantha immediately made around her waist, smiling, completely destroying the outfit...

"Oh, it was made by a friend, actually a starving artist, trying to survive with her nice creations in a harsh world," said Samantha, laughing.

Laughing too loudly, Carl dropped wine on Samantha's dress.

"Oh, sorry!"

"It is ok, it is just a dress I got for free anyway. I'm sure she can make me another one or repair this."

Samantha went to the washroom to clean the spot on the dress. It was white wine, and she was fast, the spot went away.

Andrea was there and saw Samantha walking into the washroom with the red band around her waist.

As Samantha came out of the washroom, she saw Miranda, the organizer, starting the ceremony, wearing the same dress she had, starting her speech:

"Before I start, I want to thank a new designer. The one that made the dress I'm wearing tonight. This is the most beautiful dress I ever had. Inspired by the blue of the darkest night and by the gold of the brightest stars. She could bring the light of dreams into daylight. Thank you Andrea Bettencourt. Your work is amazing!"

Andrea blushed; she did not buy the invitation, she needed the money she got for the dress to buy new materials and pay her bills.
But she got one invitation. As Miranda left the shop, on the table was an invitation with the words:
"Please come, I will be honored with your presence."

Haidji

Samantha, hearing the speech, took the red band off of her waist and still had it in her hands, as Andrea walked over to her.

"Hi, I tried to call you to tell you that I would be here too. But your phone was off. Probably no battery. I'm so happy! I sold "The Dress"! I already got calls from people asking for the same one!"

Andrea noticed the red band in Samantha's hand.

"What is that? Are you thinking about to make this artificial band on the dress? This would destroy all my concept... damage all my thoughts and hours of work."

"Me? I would never do it! I was only holding it because a good friend gave it to me."

Andrea pretended to believe it, because somehow it was her fault too. She always gave her work for free to her loved ones, thinking they would love it and value it.

Only as Samantha saw Miranda wearing the dress and speaking about it, did she realize how special it really was.

No matter how good you are, or how amazing your work is: If you don't value what you do, asking the right price for it, no one else will do it.

Sometimes, not even your best friend.

Haidji

"Life is just a class filled full with different kids doing the same or different things"

Haidji – Candles

Haidji

Candles

"What do you want to be when you grow up?"

The grandmother was outside, looking for the first spring flowers, and the girls were inside, speaking while putting their shoes on to join her.

Looking down to the floor from the top of her 6 year old height and then up again to her older sister, already 12 years old, an adult in her eyes, Maddie answered with a question: "Can I still be me?"

Followed by other questions:
"Am I not already who I am? Will I be someone else then? What will happen to me? I thought I would grow and grow and grow like you did and still be me, just taller and older. Like fruits hanging on trees. They grow and grow and grow until we pick them and eat them. Will a Giant eat me? Is Death a Giant?" asked Maddie, opening her eyes and mouth, as would she be waiting to breathe the answers in.

Shaking her head from right to left and back, while staring into Maddie's brown eyes, Lucy answered:

"No Maddie, you will still be you, you can never be someone else. We aren't fruits. No Giant will eat you, Maddie. Death... I don't know much about death. But I don't believe that Death is a Giant. I mean, what would you like to work with? Not 'who' do you want to be, but 'what' do you want to be?"

With an unemployed father and a mother who changed her work place every few months, now with a new provisional contract in a new office, this wasn't an easy question for a 6-year-old child.

"You mean, if I need to do the same thing for my whole life? Will I need to do the same for my whole life? The same thing every single day?"
"No, you don't need to do the same thing for your whole life, but maybe there is something you would like to do at first?"
Lucy was getting upset with her younger sister. Why couldn't she answer a simple question?

Haidji

Maybe because it is not a simple question, to decide what to do in your life. Neither when you are 6 years old, nor when you are 18. Find your purpose, discover your strength, you have a special gift... maybe it seems easy when you are 12 years old. But at 6 or 18...it can be very stressful to think about it. "Be yourself" is probably the best answer... if you know how to figure out who you are. If you don't, your image in the mirror, or in other people's minds, cannot help you. You need to know yourself, to know what you want in your life. If you could do only one thing you like in a day, what would you do? Maybe to know that, can help you to figure out what you like to do, and who you are, in your life.

There was not much difference for Maddie between her older sister and her parents; in her eyes, they were all adults.
After thinking for 5 seconds, which was a long time for Maddie before speaking her thoughts out, Maddie answered like a waterfall:

"I think that I will be me. I will go to University, which is a school for adults. This is what people do here. They learn things. We go to school all our life, until we are 30 and old. Then we work in an office with lots of papers and computers, which is kind like a school for older people but instead of paying for it, they pay us. The teacher is called the Boss. When you have a "Boss" you know that you are not paying for school, but school is paying for you to be there. Dad is not going to school anymore, but he learns lots of things watching TV. The government pays him for it. So it must be important too, all that he learns watching TV. We cannot speak to him or interrupt him while he does it. He works for the 'Government'. That is what I say at school, when I am asked about what my Dad does. They are impressed. So, it must be special.

After all these years working, we can retire and play again and have a second childhood when people tell us what to do, like mama tells grandma and me all the time.

I think that is what life is about.

To go to school and learn things and after all that learning we can be a kid again and play with our grandkids because Mom and Dad don't have time for it."

"I mean... you could be a doctor, a teacher, a lawyer, a fireman, a pilot or a cleaner. It is not like going to school," tried Lucy.

"In my class we have lots of different kids too. We all go to the same class.

Haidji

But we all do different paintings with the same colors. I don't see the difference. Life is just a class filled full with different kids doing the same or different things.

But if you ask me if I prefer the painting lesson or the one with the letters and sounds or to make music, I don't know. I like them all.

I think that I don't know enough to decide what I like most. I couldn't use all colors in my colors' box yet. But I still have time before the Giant comes. I think."

"There is no Giant," tried Lucy again.

"Of course there is. He is called Time. He is invisible and he eats a piece of our lives every day. He pretends to give us years, but he is taking them away. The years we get as candles on our Birthday cake are the pieces he has already eaten. Time is infinite. Huge and big. Hungry. We are like a fruit hanging on a tree or like a cake he eats."

"But what would you like to be, Maddie?"

"I want to always be me. This is what I want to be in every piece the Giant eats. In every year the Giant eats. Because I want real candles on my Birthday Cake and I don't want to give the Giant a stomachache. When the Giant eats bad cake, he throws up and this is why the Earth is destroyed in some places. It is the Giant's vomit that fell over it."

"I give up, Maddie; you are impossible... Let's go outside and see the flowers with Grandma."

And the girls went outside, and found the first Spring flowers with their grandmother; while the wind, or maybe a Giant's voice, whispered:

"May every one of your gotten years be a real candle on your Birthday Cake... to bring the light of joy to all the people you invite into your life, including yourself. "

Haidji

Haidji

"Our Present Time is the only thing we truly possess in our lives"

Haidji – Pipo

Haidji

Pipo

Luciana woke up later than usual this morning; she could not sleep much, due to the tempest outside with the lightning, thunder and wind-symphony invading her dreams, waking her up.

The sun was already almost in the middle of the sky as Luciana walked out of the house. Finally outside, she took a deep breath, still tired from her lack of sleep, and took her sandals off to walk barefoot over the green leaves. It was a hot day after an unusual tempest.

The wind must have been very strong the night before. There were green leaves all over the place, shadowing one another. Like small mosaic pieces playing with different hues of green and grey, creating images over the grass.

Luciana jumped over the images, trying to figure out which tree the leaves came from. They seemed to be fig tree leaves, but there were no fig trees around; so, the wind must have been very strong to carry them from far away. Fresh fig trees' leaves are not the lightest ones to carry away.

Between the figures created by the leaves, Luciana could see a different shade hue, a different shade of grey. It was a bird. An already fully feathered, but still baby bird, standing quietly on the ground, like a small sculpture between the leaves.

It was a small sparrow, a passer. Probably the bird fell out of its nest the night before, due to the tempest, being carried by the wind, rolling inside the big fig leaves, being protected by them. Sparrow's nests are not usually in fig trees, so the leaves must have caught the bird somewhere on the way.

It wasn't the first bird Luciana found, and it would probably not be the last. Luciana was only 14 years old but the number of birds she helped was already more than the candles she had on her last birthday cake. From time to time she came across a fallen bird, fed it, taught it how to fly, holding it on her index finger with its small feet around her finger, as would her finger be a branch of a tree. Going down slowly with her hand, is how she taught it how to fly, seeing it moving its wings, until it could let go of her finger and fly. Going back to the freedom of the world outside houses and usual human constructions. Back into nature.

It wasn't the most colorful bird, either. It was a grey sparrow. Kind of plumb and round. Cute. Like a baby bird can be.

Luciana approached with her hand slowly and took the bird off the ground; with no nest around, this bird must have rolled a long way inside of the leaves to stop there. It was alive but quiet and did not try to run away or escape from her hand. Luciana brought the bird inside and gave it some bread crumbs dipped in milk, with tweezers.

There was no wildlife center or veterinarian around. But Luciana already had experience saving lost baby birds and bringing them back to freedom again.

She knew that a baby bird aged like this one needs food every 45 minutes, all day long. So long as the sun was in the sky, she spent her day taking care of and feeding the bird, whom she called Pipo.

Pipo seemed to be round and healthy at first sight but even eating, was too quiet for a hungry baby bird. Luciana noted some blood spots on Pipo's body. Like holes with white circles surrounded by a red line of blood.

Looking closer, Luciana saw the larvae. Several blood spots showing that the bird was full with larvae from the Dermatobia Hominis, commonly known as American warble fly. Probably 5 or 6 of them in the small bird's body.

Female flies lay eggs in the nests of birds and the larvae live within the nesting material, feeding intermittently on the blood of nestlings, finding the way to enter under their skin, to feed on the living tissue of the host.

Haidji

Carefully, Luciana made some Vaseline over the larvae entrances, covering them with tape to weaken them by partial asphyxiation and then removing the tape and the larvae, one by one, carefully with tweezers.

There was not much more than skin and bones after the larvae were removed from the bird's body, but Pipo started jumping around. Feeling happier and begging for more food, or just singing and jumping inside of the shoebox that was its nest for a while, until Luciana could bring it back to the forest.

Luciana took care of the baby bird all day long, but Pipo was still too weak.

Pipo died on the same day, one hour after sunset.

Luciana was looking at Pipo, who suddenly stopped moving and fell down on the bottom of the shoebox. It was the first and only time that a baby bird she had taken care of, had died. Luciana was paralyzed for a few minutes, expecting that Pipo would stand up again, jump and sing around the bottom of the shoebox. Nothing happened.

She took the small bird's body between her hands, enclosing the bird as if it was inside of a shell, and prayed. Cried and prayed, focusing on sending all the energy she could to make the bird alive again.

Suddenly, the bird moved. Luciana opened her hands.

Made a sound, as would it be trying to stand, only to fall again inside of her hands.

Luciana could swear that the bird moved and made some sounds, and died again shortly after.

Maybe it was true, or maybe it was just her imagination. But she could swear that the bird moved again inside of her hands for few seconds, to die again. A second time. A second short life for Pipo.

It did not matter how much she prayed or cried, or how much she wanted Pipo to be alive.

The bird's body was too weak. The soul couldn't stay inside of it.

We can give a spark to someone, but if there is no fuel inside of a being, the spark goes off.

The fuel... the fuel is made by two different parts. The first part is a body healthy enough to keep a soul inside of it; and the second part is the time. The time of each being.

Why couldn't Luciana give some of her own lifetime to Pipo? Maybe because we all are timed differently. We all have our own lifetime.

But this is not all; it is also because we cannot give our future time to someone. We can't give something that doesn't exist yet; but there is a possibility to give our time to another being – we can give our present time, our love and care, to another being.

Our present time is the only thing we truly possess in our lives.

Our present time. Eternal, infinite and always available to us.

Our present moment. It is always there.

All the rest we achieve in our lives depends on what we make with our present time, how we use it, for what we use it.

Luciana found many birds before Pipo and many birds after Pipo.

She taught many of them how to fly and go back into the freedom of the world outside of human constructions again. But she never forgot the moment that Pipo, free from the larvae, was jumping and singing inside of the shoebox. And the few real or imagined seconds that the bird was alive, inside of her hands, to die again.

Was it worth it?
Yes, it was worth it to spend all day long taking care of Pipo, and to be able to give these few seconds of happiness to a baby bird.

Haidji

To give your present time to someone you love and care about is never a waste of time, because you are giving your most precious gift, wrapped in all the love you feel.

You are giving your life time.

The few moments that you can make a being smile, feel happy and loved, overcome all sadness and pain the being has, enabling it to fly free and peaceful into the unknown world after death.

Haidji

"Some people do not care about taking all the short cuts they need, to arrive at their destinations as quickly as they can – even if they destroy other people's paths in doing so."

Haidji – Lobs' Castle

Haidji

Lobs' Castle

The sun was burning her back; it was almost already red, but she did not notice it.

Stephanie was building a castle. A sand castle.

Sitting on the beach sand, focused on what she was doing, Stephanie was busy using her bucket, some old plastic beer cups she found on the sand, shells and, of course, sand itself; and she did not feel the sun hitting on her back.

The sand was grey, it wasn't a 'White sand holiday promo advertising photo catalog's beach', and in the sand around her she could see some oil spots from the recent crude oil spill. But for her that didn't matter at all. Three days she waited to finally be able to go to the beach, which had been closed due to the oil spill. An underwater pipeline ruptured, spilling thousands of gallons of crude oil into the Ocean, contaminating the beach. The more than 100,000 gallons of crude oil spilled into the ocean and covered what were once clean beaches. Cleanup crews were working to clean the beach since long before the school holidays started.

The Coast Guard said that the spill had killed one dolphin, ten pelicans and an untold number of fish and similar beings.

Stephanie wanted to help the cleaning crews in the days before, but children should not be on cleanup crews because they are more sensitive and it can cause them difficulty breathing, headaches, dizziness, confusion and nausea. Children are not immune to the effects of an oil catastrophe and its pollutants. In fact, children are more likely to have serious health problems from crude oil spills than the adults around them. They breathe more air per pound of body weight, and can absorb more through their skin than adults. This had not prevented her from trying to go to the beach every morning, waiting impatiently for when it would be possible again to play on the beach. It was weird for Stephanie to see a public, and always available, beach be shut down. It was like a freedom cut. How can a natural public space be closed? It can, when it became dangerous to human beings or animals to be there, when it became threatening to the human species.

Kids can very quickly and easily absorb toxins through their skin, or even swallow crude oil residues by transferring them from their hands to the foods they eat.

Haidji

So much as she wanted to help, it was forbidden, so, there was nothing else to do than to wait for the beach to be "friendly" again.

"What about the animals?" she thought. "I cannot go to the beach, but they are already there. How can the cleanup crew keep the baby animals out of the beach?" They could not. Many more of them would die due to the oil spill.

Volunteers working on the beach piled up plastic bags filled with blackened sand, and the stench of oil could be smelled from miles around.

Workers had made significant progress on the beach but some rocks remained coated in oil.

As the beach was starting to look a lot better than it did a couple of days ago, Stephanie was allowed to go to the beach again. The beach was again open and filled with kids, dogs, and grown ups.

Finally Stephanie could enter the beach with her small bucket and start to work on her castle.

After three days' waiting, she did not want to take a break or be interrupted; she already had the image of the castle in her mind and wanted to realize it.

The main Castle tower was made using an old bucket as a matrix. Filling it with sand, turning it upside down, knocking softly on the bucket and removing it carefully, she made the main tower; for the smaller ones, she used the plastic beer cups, some remaining drops of beer fell over the sand, but she did not care about it. She was busy, making the castle.

Around the castle she excavated a moat to protect it from enemies, not that there would be another oil spill again...

Kids playing around, people jogging on the beach, dogs, all the world noise around her was like background music. She was focused, inside of her own activity as would she be in a parallel reality... far away from all noise around her, hearing the sounds of the ocean and the sound of her own ideas and imagination.

"Now that all towers are made, I need some water," said Stephanie to herself.

Walking to the water, looking at the spots of oil on the beach, she saw a bigger spot; it was a dead baby lobster. Stephanie stopped for a while, picked it up, as would it be a shell, and brought it to her castle.

As Stephanie sat down with the dead baby lobster in her hands, she could hear some screams interrupting her:

Haidji

"Sorry, I can't stop! Sorry! Sorry!" screamed a boy, running over her castle after a rolling ball, ruining all she had done. Stephanie herself needed to jump so that the 'Ball + Boy' did not crash into her. The dead baby lobster fell over the sand and Stephanie sat down next to it, wondering if she should run after the boy, cry, scream, or give up.

Some people do not care about taking all the short cuts they need, to arrive at their destinations as quickly as they can -- even if they destroy other people's paths in doing so.

From all the work she already made, all that was left was an unrecognizable amount of trampled sand.

"Breathe deep, start over..." said Stephanie to herself.

"One Main tower and five small ones around. Like a pentagon, like a star, like a sea star."

"Hey Lobs, what do you think? I will start again and it will look better than before. Will you like it, Lobs?"

Stephanie called the dead lobster "Lobs" and started to build the castle again after the "Ball-Boy" destroyed it. She buried "Lobs" underneath the Main Tower.

"This Castle is for you, Lobs," said Stephanie.

"So no more oil spill comes over you, or over your friends. You are protected inside of your new castle."

As Stephanie was busy making it all again, some people on their way for their morning walk passed by, looking at the simple towers made by sand, saying:

"What an ugly castle, all so plain and minimalist. How can someone make something beautiful using the old beer cups on the beach? How can parents allow their kids to play with trash? It looks terrible! Someone should teach that kid how to play on the beach! She is using her bare hands to pick up the sand, no one told her about plastic shovels? Maybe she should use gloves! All the sand will go underneath her nails!"

"This is kind of sad," thought Stephanie. "These people don't like my castle and it is not even ready, they don't even wait for me to finish to spread their critiques over me... I don't need a shovel, actually it is impossible to make what I want to do with a shovel; I need to press the sand into the bucket softly with my own hand. I like it. I am sure that Lobs likes it, too."

Stephanie decided to make a battlement wall around the castle, to protect it from sea waves, invaders, oil spills ·· and stupid people critics.

Haidji

As she was working on the battlement wall, a boy stopped by, asking if he could build the wall and castle with her.

"Of course, we can make it together," said Stephanie.

The "Boy", also called Paul, alerted Stephanie that her back was getting red from the sun, giving Stephanie his own t-shirt to protect her from the sun. With the amount of sun protector his parents had made on his back, he did not need a t-shirt.

Both went together to the seaside to put some water in the bucket.

They filled the bucket ¾ with water and added some sand into it.

Stephanie showed Paul how to do it.

Grabbing a handful of wet sand, she let it drip over the matrix's figures, building up delicate spires, creating filigreed figures over the geometric figures.

The grains of sand mixed with the water falling out of her fingers fell over the forms. Looked like filigreed figures.

It was after lunchtime as they finished "Lobs' Castle".

The same people who passed by the castle in the morning came back from their walk. They stopped for a while, to admire the castle, wondering about how it was made, praising the sand construction and did not notice that it was the same one they criticized only a few hours ago.

The infinite drops of sand and water created images all over the castle, awakening the imagination of people to see their own dreams reflected in the sand. Some people had smiles, others had tears in their eyes as they stopped for a while to contemplate Lobs' Castle, as would the souls of all the animals killed by the oil spill speak through it.

Stephanie and Paul sat there, watching the sun going down over the sea before going back home for dinner, speaking about what they would make on the next beach day. Maybe they would build another castle, maybe it would be something else; nature would speak through their kid's hearts again.

No matter if someone crashes into your path and seems to destroy your dream, no matter if the world around you does not understand your goals on hearing your thoughts:
Your dream is always there, always alive inside of you.
Keep working on it, and you can go more far than you imagine you could.

Time will bring the right people into your life, if instead of running after delusions, crying, screaming or giving up, you keep serene and keep working on your dreams.

Haidji

Haidji

"You rarely know what creates
the beauty you see
in front of you."

Haidji – Hypothetical World

Haidji

Hypothetical World

The end of the week passed by slowly, until the weekend finally arrived. Covering the city with promises of rest, fun or simple happiness.

Paulette spent her morning inside her bedroom, under house arrest for a reason she did not exactly remember: maybe it was because she forgot to make her bed in the morning, or skipped lunch or dinner playing outside, or this time she was too long in the shower. For whatever reason it was, she did not remember anymore and would probably do the same things again on the following days. Happy to be able to run out of the house after lunchtime, thirsty for sunrays, she did not think about it anymore.

Swinging her legs, sitting on the branch of a tree, chewing sugar cane sliced in pieces as would they be Macdonald's chips... fake chips over a real tree leaf pretending to be a plate. No ketchup, of course. Sugar instead of salt. But chips are chips; potatoes and sugar canes are both yellow, aren't they? So, Paulette's chips were sugar canes' ones.

Paulette had to cut the sugar cane herself with a big knife she took out of the kitchen. Small knives were nothing for her; too dangerous, they fell easily out of her hand, pricking her foot; she felt safer dealing with big ones, despite other people's views about it. Apart from that, small knives made her feel like a simple thief; big ones, like a real pirate.

After slicing the sugar cane for her imaginary crew -- composed actually only of herself and some birds that don't eat chips at all -- Paulette climbed the tree, carrying the chips wrapped inside of several tree leaves, under her t-shirt. Even if the t-shirt was threaded inside of her skirt, she lost some chips on her way to the top because they slid out of the tree leaves, running over her legs, falling all the way to the ground... turning them into ants' food, inside of Paulette's mind, as she saw them falling over the ground.

Haidji

The sun going down over the city was orange due to the air pollution, but this did not make the color less beautiful for Paulette.

Some beautiful things we see are created due to not-so-good circumstances, but they are not less beautiful or magical for our eyes; at least, this is what we think until we know what creates them, but most times even after we know it.... Sometimes, to know why, increases their beauty, as would they be survivors from a post-apocalyptic time.

You rarely know what creates the beauty you see in front of you.

It is rare that you know where it comes from.

To know the facts beyond situations mostly increases their beauty, instead of decreasing it.

Paulette herself was being raised in a house that was far away from being peaceful; but even then, she had peace inside of herself.

Sitting on the branch of a tree, as high she could be.

No one could touch her, no house arrest; the sky was so close that she could almost touch her dreams.

Suddenly the world was magic; suddenly, the world was peaceful.

The orange sun was beautiful, despite the air pollution.

Sugar canes were chips; the birds around her were feeding the thirst of her soul with their melody, filling her with serenity, hope and peace.

Swinging her legs, chewing fake chips, she was on the top of the world, on the top of the highest tree she could climb, watching the sunset.

Paulette forgot the reality for a while, living inside of her hypothetical world.

Next to her, a pair of birds was building a nest; it was a couple of brown birds, Argentina's national bird, horneros. The species is monogamous and pairs remain together through the year, working on their nest. Like human couples are in some cases, both parents would incubate the eggs and feed the young. Their nests looked like a real house, made from clay. They were building their place in the world, on the branch of a tree. No birds' nests look like horneros' bird nests. They look like real small houses. Made by mud, they create a hardened shelter, oriented to face away from the wind, creating a refuge from the weather, with hard stable walls backed by the sun.

"Do I have a place in this world too?" asked Paulette, to the birds.

Haidji

"Maybe my place in the world is here, on the top of a tree, watching the sunset. Maybe one day I will build a tree house made by clay like horneros do and have my own kids inside of it." Paulette answered her own questions, watching the birds close to her, until the sun went completely down.

It was time to go back home. There was no bed story waiting for Paulette. There was no peace in the house. There was too loud music that made the house walls tremble and Paulette made her hands over her ears, trying to sleep. Or pretend to be sleeping. In a certain kind of way, she was like the orange sun... flourishing her beauty inside of a polluted world.

Yes, she skipped dinner again, and would probably be house arrested the next morning again. Cooked with too much pepper and spices, with hate instead of love, the food could not pass through her throat. She had her chips, and was full at dinnertime. All she could eat were fruits; she could not eat the food in this house. It came back and made her throw up.

As she could finally fall asleep, despite the noise, Paulette was again in her place in the world.

Inside of her own body, living inside of her dreams...

Paulette created her own world, her space, following her own intuition. Running out of the house as often as she could, she spent most of her free time on the top of a tree, swinging her legs, close to the sky of her dreams.

The people in the world can take almost everything from you.
But your place in the World belongs to yourself.
Nobody can take it away; so long as you are alive.
Even if at the beginning of your life journey it is only
The space that your soul has to be,
Inside of your body, inside of your own dreams,
A small place that cannot be measured.

But it is the first step
It is all you need to be able to walk
To be able to create your way in the World
Manifesting this place to be outside of you, too.

Haidji

"Cloistered inside the four walls of his own soul's office, searching for answers that he could find only outside of it."

Haidji – The Blue Spot

Haidji

The Blue Spot

Still in a half dream, John stood up from his bed, trying to wake up, clean his teeth, wash his face, make a coffee, change his night T-shirt against his day suit, make a second coffee, go out of the house; walking on his way to the office, thinking about all he had to do this day. Another too long – too short day in John's life.

John used to wake up around 7am, but his real day started only at 9am when he could be sitting behind his desk, working, reading over 130 emails, and answering proposals, dealing with problems. Huge problems.

Owner of a juice company, John was always dealing with problems, all day long, all 24 hours' between 9am and 7pm, like it is supposed to be for a CEO; his obligation was to deal with and to fix problems all day long. John was a problem solver and he liked it. He liked the challenges of his position.

John's mind, accompanied by his skinny body, started to work long before 9am. From 7am to 9am he was already focused on his workday. If he could remember a dream he had, it was certainly about what happened or would possibly happen inside his office. All his thoughts were about his work, 9am to 7pm; this was his real day, the one he lived in, 24 hours long, every day. Day after day after day, including nights.

There were no weekends for John. Weekends were only a change on his world Landscape. John spent his weekends at fairs -- business fairs, fruit fairs, company fairs - learning all that was there to be learned about his business, after years in the same business he wondered every time that there was always something he did not know about the fruit juice world.

Even the 1 hour break for lunch was spent thinking about what could be improved in the office or organizing his afternoon inside of his mind, speaking to employees about the company, in case he would invite one of them to join him at lunch, which happened from time to time.

Skinny by nature, more tall than large, John wasn't a fan of exercises; his exercise was the daily walk to work, the walk back home and the steps he walked around and inside the company or weekend fairs. His work already gave him enough adrenaline to deal with.

John was able to silence the world around him. Not only silence, he was able to erase the world around him, almost completely, and focus on more urgent and important things than to contemplate or see what was going on outside his Fruit Juice World; he was focused only on what happens in the one inside of his Company.

If you would ask John what happened before 9am, he could not give you an accurate answer; his mind was focused on the period between 900 and 1900. Focus, Focus, Focus, was all he thought he needed to be successful. Focus on your goal; focus on the solutions to your problems. His brown eyes were always inside of the company and never outside of it.

His mind was always working, while his heart was mostly quiet.

"Focus on what you want. Focus on what you need to do in the office. Focus on your goals and on the solution to your problems." This was the only thought John allowed himself to have in his mind when he wasn't thinking about something happening in his company; he was so used to sending other thoughts away, to be able to concentrate on it, that after a certain time of mind training, thoughts of other kinds did not even come close to his mind. There was a wall surrounded by the mantra, "Focus on what you want. Focus on what you need to do...."

Every day John walked through the same street, walking on his way to and back from work, passing through the same streets automatically, as would his body have been automated by repeating the same action everyday, passing through the same landscape.

If someone would ask him how many trees he saw on the way, which one had flowers and which ones did not have them?

How many Houses,

How many steps on the staircase in front of his house?

He could not give an answer and would try to remember...

"Stairs? Are there stairs...really?"

Every day John crossed the same Bridge on the way to his office. But he wouldn't even remember that there was a Bridge.

Maybe he would notice the seasons passing through the Landscape in front of his eyes, if he wouldn't be so focused on only one part of his day, the work part of it.

Maybe one day he would open his eyes and realize that there was a green tree smelling differently than usual, with flowers. The tree blossoms. The form and color of the flowers could make him feel excited and happy. Yes, they could, if he would be able, only for few seconds, to forget about his workday ahead of him and feel what is going on around him in the present moment of his life.

He would carry on, going his way again to work, but it would be different; he would be impressed about the perfume and inspired by the impression.

Haidji

But no, John could not see the world around him; he was focused inside of his office walls, so cloistered that nothing else existed for him anymore.

Many people want to travel, or to enclose themselves away from the world, to get ideas. To find something new in their lives, to be caught by something. Curiosity. But inspiration, new things and solutions are everywhere, around you, all the time. The world can be exciting exactly there, where you are at this exact moment. The answers you search for can be on your daily way, just waiting for you to see them. But, some people do not even look around them. John was one of these people, which was sad, because John needed a new idea urgently.

John was 'focused', or maybe better said, 'distracted' inside of the thoughts and dreams that happened only inside of his mind. Cloistered inside the four walls of his own soul's office, searching for answers that he could find only outside of it.

John arrived in his office and started to read his emails and the post mail that Susan, his secretary, left over his desk.

"Susan, is there no more mail today? I seem to receive only the same projects again and again."

"No, Mr. Swanson, there is no more mail today."

John Swanson was getting desperate. He started to doubt himself, his company, the world around him and all the rest too, because for the first time since he founded the company, the company would not be able to survive longer than a year...

Susan has a different view of life than John.

While John lived between 9am and 7pm, Susan's life happened between 7pm and 9am, which means, she was always thinking about her life outside the office and wouldn't work 1 minute longer than necessary. She was the opposite of him, but not his complementary part. Not the person he needed to be successful. Not even a person he could trust. John underestimated the value of her work and did not supervise it. Trustful and correct by nature, John could not see evil in other persons.

Sorting all his correspondence out before he arrived to the office, with not enough time for the amount of letters, bills and advertising arriving every day, Susan developed a "System" to reduce the volume of mail.

She used to reduce the mail volume, sending unnecessary post back to the post office with a stamp saying "UNREQUESTED MAIL" in blue, because red would be too unfriendly, going directly back to the sender.

Haidji

Susan decided what was necessary and what was unnecessary:

"Bills?" – Necessary.

"Job Applications?" – Necessary, but only if they were not asking for her own position, of course.

"Fruit Suppliers?" -- They already had good ones – Not needed. "We don't need new contracts and more work for me, even if your price is better and your quality is higher."

"Project ideas from dreamers thinking that they could make this a better world?" – "Unnecessary!" ...The stamp came over the mail immediately. "Who do these kids think they are? To send a letter to Mr. Swanson offering an unrequested project?" mumbled Susan, increasing the amount of the unnecessary mail.

The pain of the "Unnecessary mail" was so high that Susan ordered a box, a blue box, for it; a box she used to call "The Blue Spot".

The first time John saw the big blue box next to Susan's desk, it caught his attention. John saw everything that happened inside of his office, or at least he liked to think so.

"Was is that, Susan?"

"Oh, this is 'The Blue Spot', Mr. Swanson. I needed a box to contain all I give back to the post office; publicity, advertising, unrequested mail, etc. There is a lot of it. Amazing how many trees died for that and how many people send promotion material to us."

Her rule was 'do not work longer than 8 hours a day'; so, if she wasn't done with sorting out the mail, and all what was over it, then it was 'unrequested work and unrequested mail' -- especially on Fridays, especially bills on Fridays. "Who sends a bill to someone on Friday? Guys, do you want to destroy my weekend?" she whispered, as would the bill be for her. They should know that there was something called "weekend" -- and she needed to get ready for it, instead of sorting and proofing a bill's contents.

John's main problem was that as good as the company was doing in the summer, it was exactly as bad in the winter; people do not like to drink that amount of fruit juice in winter time, so John felt sometimes like being a seasonal worker. The idea about tea in the winter and fruits in the summer (suggested by Susan and many others) wasn't appealing. Other companies were already doing it, but for John this wasn't an option. Nor was it an option to export to the other side of the world, or import cheap feedstock from dubious suppliers. His company was a small one and all the import/export taxes were too high for him, compared to the amount of juice he could produce, and the quality of his product was of the utmost importance for him.

Summer passed by, so did autumn, and John still did not have an answer to his problem. Winter was approaching and he started to feel worried about it. For the first time he would need to fire some people.

Winter came, and one day, on the way to work, crossing the bridge before the street that would bring him directly to his company, John was thinking about how to tell his employees that some of them would have a sad Christmas present. They would get a "Blue letter" from him. He knew the meaning of a "Blue letter" from his German grandfather telling him stories, as he was a child, about the time before moving to a new country. In Germany, employees being dismissed are given "Blue Letters", "Blaue Briefe". The name refers also to disciplinary letters that children and their parents receive from their schools in the case of academic problems. The name remains, while these letters are no longer blue, but companies still used to call dismissal letters, "Blue Letters".

Walking in the middle of the too-early snow for the season, thinking about whom to give a "Blue Letter", John did not notice a blue spot. Before the bridge, on the right side. Always there, since almost a year, but now more visible. Like a big Blue Box being seen from the distance, among all the white snow.

Young kids are small; sometimes you don't see them if you are walking around looking to the sky or just facing forward. Usually you see them in the last possible second, to avoid them crashing into you while they run around changing their direction every few seconds. Not because they are hyperactive, but because they are alive, full of energy and curiosity, fearless about the world around them. But John, John had erased his impressions about the world around him almost completely, unless he would be in his company office, so he did not saw the kid coming, trying to be 'ice skating' with winter shoes over the partially frozen snowy ground on the Bridge. The crash happened.

John woke up as both of them fell on the ground and even if there was snow, the sound was like a wall breaking. The wall around his mind broke.

The child was screaming next to him, and a blue-colored juice was drawing onto the ice.

"Sir, my JUICE!"

"Excuse me", said John. "You said juice?"

"Yes, sir. My juice is gone, and now I will feel cold."

After the kid came the kid's grandmother, the one that had probably provided him the cup of juice.

"I'm sorry, sir. Kids, you know? They can't stay quiet. Come here Luke, and apologize."

"No, he did not see me, and he dropped my juice."

"Luke!"

"Ok..." mumbled Luke, looking at the blue juice slipping away, carving a small riverbed on the snow, thinking about the riverbed and rivers and fishes, and knights and dragons, because he always thought about dragons. A Knight would jump over the river and kill the dragon and...

"Luke!"

"Oh, sorry Sir, I'm sorry, but I really like this juice", said Luke, back from his battle. He was the knight and the Mister was the dragon, or his grandmother was the dragon, always telling him what to do...he still hadn't decided it yet.

"Luke!" said the woman again, reproaching the child, and then saying to John: "Sir, don't worry, I will buy him and myself another cup of juice."

"Juice? In the winter? Where can you buy juice here in the winter in the middle of this Bridge? Who buys juice in the winter? Who sells juice in the winter in the middle of a snowy Bridge?"

"There, Sir", said Luke, pointing to the Blue Spot on the right side before the bridge, before you walked onto it. He having decided to take part in the conversation, the dragon was dead, the Knight went back home, and the river was gone, inside of the snow.

For the first time, John noticed the Blue Spot, in the shape of a box, on the right side before the Bridge. It was a stand with a line of people waiting to be served and people walking with cups in their hands, drinking something. Inside of it seemed to be a young guy, student aged, with dark brown hair, selling the product, speaking and smiling all the time, with no coat.

"Wait!" said John to Luke and his Grandmother: "I can buy you a new juice, or whatever this blue stuff was, that you were drinking before crashing into me."

John walked there and waited in the line, starting to freeze, with no understanding about why people were standing in the cold to buy juice from an open stand in the middle of a snowy Landscape. It was surreal. Bizarre, and not understandable for a Juice Company owner who couldn't sell juice in the winter. Was it for free?

No, it wasn't for free and in fact, the price was even a little bit higher than usual.

John ordered one for the kid and one for himself. "Of course, I froze already and will turn into an ice stick drinking juice outside in this weather, but I need to know why people are drinking this, maybe the taste is so special that they don't mind to freeze."
John drank the blue juice and to his own surprise, the taste was good and he felt warm after drinking it.

He needed to speak to the guy that was selling the juice. To ask, who made it, where it comes from, who is his employer, what is inside of it, why he feels warm? John started to get anxious and dizzy and asked the guy if he could speak to him for a minute.

"Yes", answered the guy, introducing himself as Alex, as John introduced himself as the owner of the Juice Company on the other side of the bridge. "I'll make a short break in 10 minutes and we can speak."

Alex loved to create juices, like other people like to create perfumes or dresses.

With a small garden in his parent's Backyard, he planted his own fruit trees. He did not follow the way his parents wanted him to go, and decided to study food engineering. Seeing his passion and dedication, the family decided to support him after a year of trouble, studying at day and working at night. His father decided to use all his savings to pay for his son's tuition and allow him more time to develop his own projects.

Once he was almost finished University, he sent his resume to several companies, including the fruit companies, but no one seemed to be looking for a juice creator. His parents, both secretaries in different companies, lost their jobs, when due to the recession many companies were broken; their savings were already gone for his college education. With no other realistic solution, Alex decided to make his own small place on the bridge and sell juice for passers-by, close to his house, on the right side of the Bridge, always looking toward the Fruit Company in front of him, with certain sadness, but also a certain sureness that his goal would happen, one day.

It wasn't easy, and he did not make much money at the beginning, but he was close to home and people started to like his products. But the first winter came and things got harder. Nobody seemed to want to try or buy his winter juices. He decided to give samples for free. But nobody wanted them. His family was already living from fruit juices, that was the only eatable thing at home and Alex was considering giving up and search for any job he could find, or migrate to a better Country and send money back home. He gave himself a deadline. Three days more trying. Nothing happened on those three days and Alex decided to try one day longer. Alex was standing there again, waiting for customers who never came, and decided to make a snowman holding a cup of juice with a poster in Blue: "I drink it, would you dare to drink it too?"

After almost all day waiting for customers, Alex was almost giving up, feeling beyond anxious, depressed and desperate, breathing too fast or too slow, thinking about whether to drop all the juice over the snowman and walk away from everything, when a group of teenagers, coming back from school, decided to dare each other to see who would have the courage to try the strange blue juice.

They liked it and came back on the next day, bringing more friends with them. Some posted photos with the snowman on Twitter, Tumblr, Facebook and Instagram and in that way, the notice was spread around. Some teenagers even offered to build a new snowman every few days in exchange for a couple of juices. Alex liked the idea.

Sometimes Alex looked towards the big company beyond the bridge. He would like to work there. Every month he sent a letter with his project and idea, asking John to stop by and try his juice, being his Blue Spot so close to the company. The envelope always came back unopened, with a stamp saying "UNREQUESTED MAIL" in blue.

How can a young person make it in the world with a new idea, if no one will ask for something they don't even know exists?
John kept selling his creations on the street, kept sending letters.
Every month.
The same one.
Again and again, and they came back, again and again and again, with the same blue stamp over them.

Alex had no contacts in the juice company; no one in his family made juice before, no one worked there. There was no way to get into it through connections.
This is not the kind of story where the grandfather was a friend of the other grandfather who was the owner.
Alex's passion belonged to himself alone.
His family accepted it, without to really understand it, after seeing how much he loved it.
After the recession started, his parents became unemployed and it was his juice selling on the street that was keeping the family alive.
Not much more than that. But alive.

Haidji

Which is a lot, in a world were the biggest part of over 7.13 billion people are simply trying to survive.

As John was standing there in the cold, as Alex told him his story...he added:

"Since a few years I've been experimenting with winter fruits and fruits with thermogenic properties. To put ginger, pepper and cinnamon in everything does not help, some people don't like it. There are other ways to do it; so, I decided to try it out, find the right fruits and mixtures, and it works. The blue one is the best one for the winter, most people think that blue is the coldest color, but blue fire is the hottest one. So, I decided to try blue fruits with higher iron and thermogenic properties and mix them with other ones able to increase those properties. I call this juice 'Blue Fire'. Now, it works, and people drink my juices in the winter.

I sent you a letter every month telling you about my project and you never answered. Did you ever receive them? They always came back unopened, with a stamp saying UNREQUESTED MAIL."

John was feeling excited, anxious, dizzy, guilty, overwhelmed. The answer he was searching for was right there. Since over a year, trying to get into his office. So close to his hands but slipping away, month after month; falling into the wrong Blue Spot, erasing the right thing, from his life.

"Alex, would you like to work for my company as a product developer, after all?" he asked Alex.

"Yes, with two conditions."

"Conditions? What conditions?"

"I want to keep the Blue Spot and be here part-time; I like to know what people think about my products and I like the people I see here every day.

I want a job for my parents too. They are depressed and sad, feeling worthless at home."

"I accept your conditions," said John, giving Alex a handshake. You can start tomorrow and bring your parents with you and we can search for an employee who likes to be here part-time, in your "Blue Spot".

Going back to his company's office, John delivered only one Blue Letter.

To Susan.

Unexpected by John, she wasn't really sad about it, because even with her limited actual work time, she could apply for unemployment benefits.

Alex's parents, after a job interview, were hired as a secretarial couple.

All mail was now checked, one by one, and the ever-increasing amount made them find an intern to help with the work.

After one year, John offered Alex a Partnership.

"Blue Fire" became famous -- so famous that they changed the company's name into it and no one remembered the old name of the company anymore. "John's Orchard" was never appealing anyway.

One day, standing in front of the "Blue Spot" with Alex, John saw Luke and his grandmother again. Luke was already finishing High School, but his family had no money for college. John and Alex created the "Blue Fire" Scholarship to help Luke, and every year after it, they offered sponsorships to young adults for their College Degree. In case they were into the same business, also an internship and a possible job in the company; and if not, well, Blue Fire was also becoming a sponsor for science projects and working with other companies.

If you really want something and light the fire inside of you, soon or later, it will come to you.

Sometimes you need to crash, to break the walls around your mind and be able to see the world around you, trying to give you all answers you are searching for.

Many people want to travel, or to enclose themselves away from the world, to get ideas. To find something new in their lives, to be caught by something. Curiosity. But inspiration, new things and solutions are everywhere, around you, all the time. The world can be exciting exactly there, where you are at this exact moment. The answers you search for can be on your daily way, just waiting for you to see them.

"You can't stand up while you're still falling."

Haidji – Based on a True Story

Haidji

Based on a True Story

Being the third of five kids, there should not be so many expectations on her.

But things in life aren't always the way we expect them to be, or what we think they should be; so, the expectations were there. Anika knew from childhood on that success was a must in her family. For everyone, and each child carrying the weight of her parent's surname, growing up inside the same house. It wasn't an unconventional, noble or rare surname. The surname was Smith, a common one, but they were raised and treated, as would they be the only Smith family in the world. They were "The Smiths".

All the kids needed to be successful, to compensate their parents' hard work by raising them and bringing their name from the mass of people in the society sharing the same five letters in their ID's, to the surface of a new level.

From being a simple Smith into being an acknowledged part of "The Smiths."

Each kid's school uniform was ironed every evening for the following school day, and the white shirt was worth a washing powder commercial on the TV.

Lawrence, Anthony, Anika, John and Karen were worth a Christmas card made by Hallmark or Papyrus.

But not all kids can grow up accomplishing their parents' wishes and expectations of them. Kids have their own dreams and expectations. When parents try to force them in a certain direction, it can be difficult for a child to discover what they really want to do in, and with, their lives.

Lawrence and Anthony followed the family path and were already working with their parents. More or less happy about their lives.

John, with his strong will, rebelled and decided to go his own way and travel to Bali with his boyfriend, to find himself and decide what to do with his life between smoking pot and overcoming his 'need' for ironed towels, becoming a defender of using the same clothes all week, having a shower every 2 or 3 days in the name of love and compromise (only because his boyfriend would move out if he wouldn't do it), and protecting the environment using no shampoos or soap.

Karen found her way being a nurse as she failed to enter Medical school; secretly this was what she wanted anyway and the only reason she did not enter Med school was because instead of working to increase her grades, she did her best to decrease them, to avoid the painful explanation of not going to the best University in the country in case she entered another, failing all applications and trying her parents' second option without letting them know that it was her first one. "Oh, so sad, I am so devastated, I'm not so intelligent like you expected me to be, but, I could do my best to be a nurse, Dad." Crying outside and laughing inside, she saw her dream come true. Karen became a nurse.

Anika? Well, Anika...

Some tasks stay with you, even when there is no one other than yourself to accomplish them on a daily basis. Habits.

Years later, still always wearing freshly ironed shirts and suits, Anika, already 28 years old, still did not know what to do with her life to feel fulfilled and happy.

She had lots of examples, lots of people to be inspired by, apart from her parents, friends and closest family.

She read lots of books, subscribed and took part in lots of workshops, courses and seminars. Anika made all her life decisions based on what should be the best for her.

She tried to have rooms like Walt Disney, think like Steve Jobs, be fearless like Donald Trump, and charismatic like Oprah. She read all the books about being successful.

Focusing on every detail, her practice was doing ok, but it wasn't the "hit" in the city, not even the "hit" in the building, even if the building was composed of three different floors and only two law practices. Between herself and the nerdy looking other lawyer, who mostly had spots on his shirts, never brushed his dark blond hair and managed to keep his clients waiting at least 15 minutes for a scheduled appointment, she was the 'number 2'. Tom Clarson managed to be more successful than Anika Smith. But apart from her parents, no one else cared about it. Anika was a very nice person and average nice looking young lawyer; she took care of her cases, the best she could, but the lack of passion or natural ability to deal with judges, other lawyers and litigation made her clients give her only the easy cases, the ones where they wouldn't lose much, in case she wouldn't make it happen. Most of the time her research was so deep, that she wasn't sure anymore about her own arguments. She had trouble to take and defend a side; for her, everyone could be right, depending on the point of view, which wasn't easy for accomplishing the challenges of her profession.

Haidji

Anika read lots of books, not only about her profession, and made sure to read all book reviews before choosing a book, because this is how she was told to do it; even if she was more the kind of person who would prefer to read book reviews after reading the book, because she knew how easy it could be to influence her decisions and make her pick the wrong one, based on someone else's taste or way of thinking. But she followed other people's advice. She tried to follow everyone else's advice and got lost and confused sometimes, without knowing what to do. To avoid it, she tried to read books that followed the same line of thinking, for a certain period of time, leaving the crisis for later by reading only later the opposite way of seeing things.

The first Barbie she had, she got because her cousin had one and liked it so much. Because all girls had Barbies and she should have and love one too.
She played with it, but she did not like it.

University was picked upon Uncle Jonathan's advice. Uncle Jonathan was her mother's younger brother. "Look at your parents, Anika. They are both lawyers, you should follow their path and advice." She followed the already-prepared way for her to go, and got her own practice as a graduation present. A small one, a good way to start before proving that she could, one day, be associated with her parents' practice, where her two older siblings were already working, while the other two kids escaped the family karma, turning themselves into simple Smith's, falling out of the "The Smiths" family weapon.

If someone would ask Anika about her university time, she would describe it as years of punishment and for being able to tolerate a certain amount of masochism trying to digest all the information she got, being a good student, a good daughter and a good example as a human being. Suffering, but being happy to accomplish the expectations of her closest family and friends.

Every class was painful, but she did it, with the best results, remembering only good moments, the ones when she drank a little bit more than she was allowed and decided to stand up in the middle of the night and cook with whatever she had inside of her fridge, to serve whoever was around to eat it, creating good memories for the nights of other students.

Exhausted and happy after some bottles imbibed and a nice meal shared with colleagues and friends, is when Anika could fall asleep peacefully, inside a dark room.

Haidji

For her, a dark room was the best place to be.

Quiet, peaceful, no disturbing images or voices.

Not even music; this was the best place to think about whatever it is.

Where no one else, not even a sound, could give her advice about what to do with her life, or what to think about, or how to think at all.

After those nights, in the next morning, in front of the mirror, using a mantra as a make-up to her hangover, she repeated to herself:

"Be like, get inspired on, look like; this is the correct and most successful way to do things."

Predictable like the presence of sand on a Caribbean beach, staying in the same building, having common interests and being both single with no time to think about dating other people, Annika Smith and Tom Clarson came closer; unpredictable, is that it was real love, even if it was built over a convenient situation.

It all started with a coffee he brought her one morning, after saying "hi" for the twentieth time crossing each other's way going in or out of the building or in the corridor, stairs or around the corner.

Tom took some time to have the courage to bring her a coffee, but she smiled back every time he spoke to her and sometimes she stayed longer in front of him, running her fingers through her long black hair as would she consider to say something more than "hi", suddenly flashing her eyes, looking down, blushing and turning back abruptly into another direction.

The fourth time he brought her a coffee was followed by lunch together. After a few times having lunch, they jumped into dinner... it took a couple of dinners together for both to realize they were dating. After they realized their feelings for each other, things started to rush in their natural way.

After 6 months' dating they moved in together and one night, with a bottle over the considered allowable number for a night, Anika stood up and decided to recover her University ideas about a meal, instead of ordering Italian, Indian, Chinese, Greek or Japanese take-away food. Anika cooked for Tom.

Even having a considerable amount of alcohol cheating his senses, Tom found it amazingly tasteful, different, innovative, and marvelous.

Anika smiled... "You had too much alcohol, Tom."

But, there were leftovers, and eating them in the next day, not hungry at all, recovering from the hangover, with a strong headache, the meal was still amazingly tasteful.

With the support of Love, Anika closed her practice and turned it into a space for a future restaurant. She was disinherited by her parents in respect of their permission of her being part of "The Smiths." Apart from their own disappointment ‥ one kid more being not impressed about their profession, disappointed that it happened to one more child ‥ it made them start to consider what they did wrong in their education. They were the type of people who believed they have the property rights in, and control of, what to do with a present; while the kids should get only possession of it. Theoretically. The practice was in Anika's name, she could do what she wanted with it, according to the law. But not according to her parents; even being top lawyers, possession and property rights were different for them, when it was about their presents to their own descendants. They were parents' theoretical rights. The ones that were almost never acknowledged or recognized by kids.

Anika followed her gut and the world's law. It was her practice. She closed it and worked on it, to turn it into a restaurant. She could invite all her clients to the opening. Tom could invite all his clients too. There would be new clients for Tom and new clients for her. They would double their clients, working in different fields. Tom could take over her cases and Anika could get lots of new clients for tea or coffee, maybe even lunch, while they were waiting for his appointments.

It was perfect.

Anika started: she used all her savings, read all the books she could about cooking, restaurants, kitchens, participated in all classes and seminars from the best chefs, trying to copy each one's technique into perfection and seeing her masters as examples she should follow.

After a year, she managed to have it all and decided to make a 'proof evening' for her friends.

Unfortunately Tom wouldn't be present, busy taking a seminar to get continuing professional development credits.

The proof dinner would be on his last seminar day and he could arrive only at the end of the dinner, but maybe still able to enjoy the last minutes of her victory.

Anika prepared everything very carefully, following the advice of the best chefs in the world. Taking care of every detail according to all the seminars, workshops, courses she took part in and all the books she read.

Her friends arrived anxious for her dinner, among them some colleagues from the university times, yearning for one of her magic meals.

As they started to eat, Anika could see in their expressions: It was ok, but there was nothing amazing. There were skills displayed, but the passion was gone. The magic wasn't there anymore. Anika failed. She failed as a lawyer, and she failed as a cook.

Anika got depressed and did not go home that night; she did not know how to face Tom, who had already sent her uncountable SMS texts about his flight being delayed and asking how the dinner went, and the last one, congratulating her on her success...
She couldn't answer. She tried, but she couldn't. She wanted to allow him some minutes more of happiness before crashing his expectations of her skills.

Sitting alone in the middle of her newest kitchen, already way ahead of the normal amount of alcohol allowed in a social or non-social environment, Anika, staring at an apple that seemed to be calling for her, decided to make an apple pie or maybe baked apples, she wasn't sure about it. Something with apples. Whatever it will be, she would do it.

Of course, like always, she used the biggest knife she could find; small knives were for cowards or kids.

The apple always rolled away as she tried to cut it. "Damn apple! Do you want a fight? Ok. I will get you!" said Anika, while she took the apple in her left hand, the knife in her right hand and with the apple in her left hand she decided to cut it, taking a thrust to do it, as would she be something between a baseball player launching a ball, a fencing fighter, or just an angry girl trying to win a tiny battle after losing the war. The tiny apple battle turned into the war itself. A new war. "Damn apple!"

With all her anger, disappointment and pain concentrated in her knife, as would the knife be an extension of her hand and a new part of her own being, she went one step back with her right foot and then thrusted forward while making a fighting movement with her right arm, screaming some unrecognizable sounds, the meaning of which would be something like: "I got you."

Anika lost her balance.

She tried to stand up as she noticed it but,

You can't stand up while you're still falling.

The apple fell on the floor and the knife, still being part of her being, fell over the apple, cutting it into cross-sections so fast, and sticking into the floor.

Using an inappropriate vocabulary that would, if her parents could hear it, disinherit her forever (not only from being part of "The Smiths", but from being seen as their daughter), Anika let the knife remain stuck in the floor, as would a member of her body be mutilated, and crawled over the floor searching for the apple pieces.
She found one half of the apple, keeping it inside of her left hand, while she was searching for the other half.

Tom came in and found Anika sitting on the floor, looking inside the apple's halves, crying; and he came closer slowly. Slowly and carefully like people are after an Earthquake, just in case there will be more shocks. He thought she would still be celebrating and had flowers in his hands.

"Tom, look..." she said.

"Stars...there are stars inside the apple, I never saw them before."

I will make a dish based on the stars inside an apple and call it Fencing between Stars ...I will make it..." And she started to cry again, exhausted.

"They are amazing, Anika," said Tom, pulling the knife out of the floor, bringing it into a safe place, the first drawer he saw, the napkins' one.

And quickly looking for a glass vase big enough for the flowers, as would they have always been there.

Tom carried Anika home, trying to figure out what happened, between her hiccups, vomiting attacks and tears.

He gave her a bath, made her a tea and played her preferred CD to help her fall asleep, singing according to the melody. Tom was a disaster as a singer, but Anika was so exhausted and drunk that his voice was the safety she needed to fall asleep. Speaking or singing or simply holding her, he brought her to the land of recovery and dreams. A deep sleep.

In the next day, Anika spent her day cutting apples and other vegetables in the same way she liked to read books. Without to care about what others would do.

As would each element inside her kitchen tell her its own story, inspiring her about what to do with it, she changed the position of the tables, the color of the plates and all the decorations.

Haidji

And prepared a new meal for her friends. Without alcohol in her system while cooking, she managed to recreate her university days, as would she be working for a Ph.D. A Ph.D. in cooking.

This time, she could see the spark of the stars in her friends' eyes... and she was ready to officially open her restaurant.

As predicted, most of her clients became Tom's ones and most of his clients became her new ones, bringing new people to both sides.

After she got her first Michelin star, a hallmark of the finest dining quality for restaurants around the world, her parents decided to forgive her for closing her practice by welcoming her to "The Smiths" again.

But it was too late; Anika and Tom had already privately married shortly after the disaster with her first dinner, without her parent's presence, and she had changed her surname to Clarson.

All her siblings came to the marriage and John washed his hair for the event.

Anika welcomed her parents to come to the restaurant and be part of their lives, keeping a healthy distance, with no stalking opinions and advice. A non-spoken kind of verbal agreement full of clauses without hints, but with direct meanings, shown by actions, reactions and moves, was accepted by both parties.

Anika's life was based on a true story. A different one by every moment, or by every book she read or seminar she took part in. Based on lots of true stories accomplished and lived by other people, but never on her own one, until the Apple Battle happened.

All she could be, trying to be like, get inspired by, look like...was to be a reflection of someone else in life's mirror.

Being someone else's reflection in a mirror, you fail to see or show the beauty of your own soul.

You fall deeper and deeper while climbing into a precipice, after someone else's light.

Someone else's light can bring you into the center of things, deep inside the knowledge, but there is certain point in your path where you need to find and follow your own light, to be able to reach the stars.

Stars.

Sometimes you need to find them inside of apples, after a war, to be able to see them inside of yourself, too.

Haidji

"We feel the measure of things according to how high we can count.

The weight, we feel, according to how much we can carry.

All that is over our capacity to understand, turns into the infinite, no matter how old we are."

Haidji – The Pine Tree

Haidji

The Pine Tree

White over white, snow covers the landscape while infinite new snowflakes are falling from the sky, increasing the amount of white for the viewer's eyes.

The only other colors between all the white and bluish-white ice were the yellow light inside a house window and the green top of an old Pine Tree situated halfway up to the top of the Mountain.

It was as would the Pine Tree be watching a house placed halfway between itself and the end of the Mountain, looking inside its window.

All the Pine Tree can see through the window are kids, decorating a Christmas tree with several ornaments. John and Katie, his younger sister, joking, teasing each other and feeling very busy decorating the tree, while their mother brings several delicacies to the table.

It is almost Christmas Eve.

Looking through the window, John can see all the way up to the top of the Mountain, and feels as would the big Pine Tree, halfway up between the house and the top of the Mountain, be watching him. For John, the Pine Tree was like the Mountain Guardian. Not that there were no other trees – there were so many that the boy couldn't count them – not just because of being five years old and able to count only up to fifty, but because they seemed to be infinite, like the hairs on his head. One day he tried to count his own hair, but he couldn't. They were more than fifty. The trees are more than fifty too, so they are a thousand, or infinite.

This Pine Tree is the highest of all the other trees on this mountain and probably the oldest one around. Probably 1000 years old, John used to think, for John, able to count until 50 but only with effort and feeling tired afterwards, 1000 and infinite was the same. The real age of the Pine Tree was around 2024 years; it wasn't a *Pine Pinus longaeva*, the longest-lived life form on Earth whose oldest known individual is already more than 5000 years old, but it was an ancient tree and for John there wasn't much difference between 60, 1000, 2024 or 5000.

We feel the measure of things according to how high we can count.
The weight, we feel, according to how much we can carry.
All that is over our capacity to understand turns into infinite, no matter how old we are.

Like our problems, unless we make the effort to understand them, the scarier, bigger and heavier they are.

Once we learn to understand them, we can find a solution and, in case there is none, it is at least easier to live with them knowing their real sizes.

The Pine Tree observes the house year after year; the light it sees through the window is the only light in the middle of a dark winter evening. "I would like to experience a Christmas night inside of this house", thinks the Tree. "Even if afterwards I could never come back to the top of the Mountain and watch the kids rolling down it with sleds or skis. Every year, something magical seems to happen at this house. They all sing, they are all happy and they wait for a certain Santa Claus, whose arrival I always miss."

Wondering about what could be so special happening inside this house – to justify the sacrifice of a baby tree every year passing by, to celebrate love and life – the Pine Tree tried to move, as would he be able to walk down the hill and knock on the door.

But fixed in the Earth by its roots, the Pine Tree was not able to walk down and see things more closely, so he kept watching the house from the distance, seeing only the yellow square spot called a window, and only a small part of this family's life.

Before the end of this day, John decided to climb the Mountain again and to go down on his sled.

Once more, stopping by the Pine Tree, he looked up to the big tree, remembering how he used to sit in its shadow in summertime, reading a story or just running in circles around it, singing, screaming or making noises from some foreign language available only in his imagination.

The Pine Tree seemed to be so lonely now, in the middle of the snow. Even surrounded by 'infinite' other trees, it seemed to be lonely and kind of sad.

"Oh, I would like to take you home with me! You would love to see Santa! Not that I could ever see him, only grown-ups can see him. But you are so big; you would see him for sure! You look so lonely here," said John.

Haidji

Unexpectedly, John hugged the Pine Tree. Or part of it...it was bigger than the circumference his arms could make. So he made a circle around it, hugging it all, sliding his arms around it to make sure it was a complete hug. He repeated it 3 times; just to make sure the hug went all the way around. Going around all of it with his arms. It felt good.

"Merry Christmas, Pine Tree! I hope you can see Santa."

A pinecone fell, and some sap fell after it, onto the snow.

Falling over the cold snow, the sap turned into the shape of a snow star.

John picked up the star and the pinecone, and the wind, passing by through the pine tree branches, seemed like laughter.

John brought the star home and placed it on the top of the Christmas tree. He gave the pinecone to Katie and she painted it with different colors, placing it somewhere on the tree.

As the kids placed these new ornaments on the Christmas tree, something. Happened:

From halfway up to the top of the Mountain, the Pine Tree could now see the whole room, and be inside the house, being part of the Christmas night: part of the tree's soul came in the frozen star. The Pine Tree could now feel the warmness and peace of Christmas, and be part of it.

Maybe the Pine Tree saw Santa; maybe it didn't see him.

But it was able to be part of Christmas inside the house, as it had wanted to be. Without having to die for it, or being ripped out of the earth to enter the house.

It is possible for a soul to be in two (or more) places at the same time?

We can't rip ourselves out of where we created roots and be everywhere.

Even then:

Many of us are in several places at Christmas time; we are in all the places we send a card, a present, a thought, good wishes and/or love. We are in the past, as memories of the ones we cared for; and in the future, depending on what we do now and in the present time.

Like the Pine Tree, we are guardians of those we love, taking care of them, without losing our own lives and roots.

Through love, we are able to be everywhere, in this magical time called Christmas Time.

Haidji

"Don't cry before the milk is spilled—maybe when it happens you already turned into a vegan, so you wouldn't drink it anyway."

Haidji – Flowers

Haidji

Flowers

The silver transverse flute was lying quietly over the table, as Judith left the house.

Long ago... was the last time she could play her pain away, into a melancholic melody. Now it reminded her of the tones she used to play, to scare her pain away.

Sometimes tears escaped from her soul into her eyes, usually while attaching the tools to her hands with plaster and gauze, to be able to work on her newest jewelry piece for her current university semester; tears she tried to hold until they turned into willpower and smiles, remembering the stories about "Aleijadinho", an amazing Brazilian sculptor who could only create his statues by attaching tools to his hands, being incapable of moving them. Son of a Portuguese man and an African slave, Aleijadinho's life turned into legend, because of his statues. Judith, with her red hair and Irish parents, was neither Portuguese nor African, and did not even know exactly where Brazil was. But she felt closer to Aleijadinho than most of his countrymen would ever be able to feel.

Feeling special for a moment, every time she worked on her pieces after her friend Liana told her about him, she decided to do the same: live in the moment and be able to finish as many pieces she could, in the time she had. Who knows? No doctor could ever tell her how long it would take for her nerves to fade away.

"The future? Who knows, Judith", Liana used to say. "There are 3D prints you can design in the computer, you can go into product design and create amazing stuff anyway. No one ever knows what the future will bring. Don't cry before the milk is spilled—maybe when it happens you already turned into a vegan, so you wouldn't drink it anyway."

Liana could always cheer people up, she thought, going slowly down the steps—there was no elevator in the building and her apartment was on the second floor. She was going out to meet Liana for lunch at the University Cafeteria. Her nerves were dying, but her mind and soul were alive.

Some people compare your body to a car, carrying your soul through life.

But, it isn't the same. You can have none, one or many cars in your life.

Your body? You have only one. Once your soul gets into it, it stays there from your first until your last day. You need to deal with what you get. Some changes are possible due to the state of modern medicine and science, but you can't crash it and buy a new one.

Liana was also the one friend who cut Judith's food, pizza, steaks and difficult meals for her, exchanging her plate with hers in social situations after doing so, so no one could notice her incapacity to hold a knife and fork anymore.

Haidji

Judith's polyneuropathy was taking its course, slowly and surely. Weakness, numbness, and burning pain, affecting her autonomic nervous system; so, there was no time for tears. Only to live and smile. With a big smile on her pale face, Judith left her apartment to slowly go down the steps on the way to her car. She could still drive her car. She could walk. So, she could smile too. "Snow Tempest? Good that I have a car and can drive. I would take a week to arrive at the tempo I walk now," murmured Judith to herself, walking out of her apartment.

Liana entered the Cafeteria, looking for Judith at each table. She wasn't there yet.

Still looking for Judith, even knowing she had not yet arrived, Liana saw Renate, another girl, crying loudly, sitting in front of a plate. It was a plate for a full meal and she was crying in front of her plate and one already empty beer can. "What happened, Renate?" asked Liana.

"Oh, it is so terrible, you know."

"What happened?" asked Liana again, leaning over Renate while pulling her long brown hair together with an elastic she used to carry on her wrist, to avoid it falling over Renate's tears.

Renate wasn't the beauty ideal or the friendliest girl in the place; kind of arrogant, with her overweight size, she was mostly cold and distant.

To see her crying wasn't something a person expected, not even on a Snow Tempest day.

Liana asked her for the third time about what happened.

"It is so difficult, and it is why I turned overweight, cranky and sad. It is the reason why I eat so much and why my life is so miserable."

Liana expected to hear a crushing story, to explain so many tears.

The story came like a bomb. It was a crushing story.

Renate told her: that as she was about nine years old, at lunchtime (they used to have lunch at school in those days), her teacher forced her to eat the soup. She screamed at her and she could not leave the room before eating at least half of her soup.

"It was horrible, I did not want to eat and she forced me to eat the soup."

Haidji

Tears rolled down Renate's face. "This is why now I eat so much and this is why I am so fat and miserable. I kind of liked the soup, but I did not want to eat it, I did not want to eat it and she, she, she forced me. Now I am fat and think I need to eat everything all the time. All the time." Explained Renate, between hiccups and tears.

Overcoming the shock of the situation, after losing her voice for a while, Liana hugged Renate, explaining that it was all Ok now, no one was forcing her to eat anymore, all was fine. She did not need to eat everything all the time...

Do people create problems when they don't have some? Or to awaken compassion in others, do they imagine problems or fabricate explanations for the results of their own choices and behaviors in life?

Liana was still calming Renate down as Brigitte entered the place, all upset and speaking loudly, putting her purse on the table, not even noticing Renate's tears still rolling down her face. Not even noticing Judith trying to open the door to enter the room, she had slammed the door against Judith's face after she entered, making Judith fall.

"OMG, OMG, this was so terrible and enlightening!" said Brigitte, almost shouting at them.
"What happened?" asked Liana, while still trying to calm Renate down.

"You won't believe it! It is so terrible. I came here by bus. A woman was aggressive, very aggressive; she tried to take my purse. It was so painful."

"Are you ok? Did she hurt you?" asked Liana, as more persons, hearing the dramatic words, approached the table to check on her.

"There were eight people on the bus, apart from me, the seven other people started screaming at the woman and she needed to leave the bus, it was so enlightening. I don't know why these bad things happen to me every day, as wouldn't I have already enough bad stuff going on in my life.

I can't go to class today. I need to recover from all this. Maybe I will need a week or a month to recover from it."

"Oh, you poor girl, but, your purse is here, didn't she take it?" asked Sami, sitting at the next table.

"No, but she tried. Someone tried to steal my purse. This is so terrible."

People were so busy hearing Brigitte's story that no one noticed Judith entering the place. She had taken probably five minutes to stand up, open the door and enter, but she could hear the loud story, and she approached the table.

Haidji

"Yes, it was enlightening," said Judith. "You and eight people in the bus. A woman attacks you. Seven people, I mean, ALL the other passengers in the bus immediately help you and the bad one is thrown out of the bus. No one knows if she was hungry, poor, or just a common thief, or maybe slipped and held onto your purse in order not to fall. But everyone helped you. Is it what happened? Seven good people weren't enough for you to be thankful?"

For a moment a flash of hatred crossed Brigitte's eyes, aimed in Judith's direction.

"Seven wasn't enough for you to be thankful?" repeated Judith.

"How dare you to ask me for details? When I say it was terrible, it is because it was. It is not important if she just slipped and was holding onto my purse to stand up again, or if she was trying to steal it. These are details, small, stupid, unimportant details. No one should touch my purse without my permission. She is bad and destroyed my day, week and month."

"Brigitte, you are responsible for your thoughts and actions and the creation of your destiny," said Judith.

"Life is what you make of it.

I am tired about hearing every day how miserable you make your own life to be, instead of seeing the beauty of it. How do you dare? How do YOU dare? Eight people in a bus with you. One maybe bad, seven good. Shouldn't you feel blessed and protected?

Was it bad that seven people protected you? That you still have your purse and the bus stopped to throw the woman out? Do you need now the 'after it happened protection' of the whole world, for something that was immediately fixed?"

Before Judith had spoken, Liana was already hugging and consoling Brigitte. But while Judith was speaking, Liana let Brigitte fall out of her hug, letting her slide into the arms of others who had come to the table, her new victims... also called supporters.

Liana did not want to live in a world where to be forced to eat a plate of soup as a 9-year old child turns into a lifetime traumatic event, and where seven good people are ignored because someone needs to feel like a victim, no matter what, maybe even accusing an innocent person when there was no one else to blame in her day.

Between hugging Brigitte and letting go of her, Liana was trying to understand the human capacity to feel, create or overcome pain, with the pain sometimes increasing to an incomprehensible point. The pain wasn't there before; it was created from almost nothing.

Brigitte kept telling—recycling—her story, sending hateful looks into Judith's direction, all the while ignoring Judith's words.

Leaving Brigitte with her supporters, Liana and Judith moved to another table, joining Peter, Sami and Clare, other students, people with life's scars inside or outside, but who carried a positive attitude towards life.

Sometimes,
There is nothing...but if you work on it, something will become.
Something that can grow and isn't just part of yourself anymore, but affecting each and every one around you, taking it's own way.
Who is responsible?

A woman had slipped on a bus and tried to remain standing, by holding onto a purse.
She was accused of being a thief, thrown out of the bus, and needed to walk to her destination.   She missed her job interview.   A few days after, she got another interview somewhere else, and got the job.   If the missed one would have been better, she would never know; but, in her mind it would have been, and she thought about it from time to time.
So... she decided to buy a car.

Liana offered to pick up the plates for herself and Judith, quickly cutting Judith's steak, as would it be her plate, and then exchanging the plates after doing so. Of course Peter, Sami, Clare and many others knew about it, but they all pretended they did not, so as not to embarrass Judith. They were all worried about Judith's future, but decided to support her and live in the present time. There were many other lunch meetings and beautiful moments during their university time.

Persons are like flowers, in all different types and colors. Some are happy, like summer flowers; others are strong like edelweiss, adapting to cold and difficult high altitudes.

Haidji

But some people are a beautiful flower full of poison, conquering you with its apparent fragility and sweetness. As would it be alone in a field full of danger, when the only danger for the field, and for the world around it, is the flower itself. A sweet flower full of poison, playing by its own rules, caring only about its own pleasures; not even survival, just pleasures, no matter who gets killed for it.

Sometimes the problem with bad people is their good side, which catches you. Their apparently captivating, charming, sweet side.
Some humans are like poison flowers.
But there is a difference.
Flowers do not have a choice.
Human beings do have.

We all have the talent and inner beauty to be an amazing flower.
If someone choses to be a poison one, it is sad.
But it is her or his own choice to decide how to deal with a situation; and it is our own choice to support it or not.

To be watchful and alert to the details where the truth lies.
But without forgetting that even if there is nothing remarkable, there is a minimal detail; if you work on this detail, it becomes something and this something runs out of your hands, affecting other peoples lives, for good or for bad.
You and only you are responsible for the consequences of your actions, failures and successes.

Life is what you make of it.

Sometimes, all you have to do is move to another table, and stay away from poison flowers, no matter how beautiful and sweet they appear to be.

So that edelweiss and other amazing flowers can become part of your life's bouquet, bringing you joy and happiness.

"Your parents aren't always your soul parents;
your children, not always your soul children."

Haidji – The Soul's Children

Haidji

The Soul's Children

Being lighter than air itself, with no need of wings, she walked around in circles through the sky, looking down to Earth.

As she looked down she saw two stars, very distant from each other and said:
"But... they are so far away from each other, I can't choose only one of them, and I like both."

The Angel said to her:
"Better you choose other stars; these two will meet only later on in life, can't you see how far away from each other they are at this moment, each one of them living its own life, not even knowing about one another's existence?"
"It doesn't matter... I will wait," answered the girl.

"She is so beautiful, have you see her eyes? How can she be so serious and so funny at the same time? It seems as would she be dancing while she walks... and he, have you noticed his smile? It is as would he be tickling me every time he smiles." She laughed, kissing her own hands and throwing the kisses in both directions, kisses falling over the stars and, at the same time, in different parts of the world.

"Do you think I look like her?" She wondered, and tried to walk like her... above the clouds, speaking to herself because the Angel had been gone for some time.

Then she saw a boy sitting with his head between his hands and asked him:

"What are you doing? Why are you holding your head between your hands?"

"I'm waiting. I'm waiting for my chosen stars to meet each other. But it seems it will never happen."

"Which ones?" she asked, thinking that they will maybe be some boring ones, because she had picked the better ones already. She asked just out of curiosity and sympathy, politeness.

"Look... you see, they are those ones... and showed her the two distant stars that seemed to be beginning to approach each other, then to take different paths again. "Can you see? She is the most beautiful of all, and he, can you see? Do you think there can be a better one? Have you seen him fighting? His sense of humor? He is the strongest of all and has secrets he will tell only to me."

"But, they are the same as mine!" and her face lit up.

She did not need to wait alone any longer. They began to run after each other and play while expecting the infinite time to pass by, the time that never seems to pass by while you are waiting for something.

Haidji

They laughed every time the stars seemed to walk in one another's direction, jumping and running between rainbows; and they cried every time life took them into opposite directions again.

The Angel came to ask them if they had already chosen their stars.

"Yes, of course, the same ones we said before. They are approaching each other, can you see?"

The Angel's mien turned serious and greyish.

"No, it is not all right, you should choose at least three possibilities, three different possibilities. Not just one. You need to consider everything to fulfill your purpose on Earth. From your DNA to your environment. From the day you are born until the day you should come back. Stop walking together as would all be chosen, well and certain; and go choose the other possibilities."

The children cried, shouted, flounced. After all that, they wept in silence; they did not want to choose other stars. They wanted only those ones.

They gave each other their hands while crying and their tears, running out of their eyes, sliding down their arms, landed on their hands' palms, and glued their hands together in an almost eternal form of tantrum.

The Angel used his hands to separate their hands, demanding that they go apart and chose other stars.

They were placed in different places and ordered to look for other stars, but they managed to flee and to find each other again.

Crying again, watching their chosen stars, their hands glued again.
The Angel found out they were together again, with their glued hands, and asked them if they had already chosen other possible stars.
They answered him: "Yes, we have already chosen; we stay together and we picked the same ones." They did not want others.

The Angel swung his sword between their hands to separate them. They were hurt; blood came out of their wounds. Again, they were taken to different places to choose other stars.

Once again, even before their hands' wounds stopped bleeding, they fled and met up, to see together the stars they loved, and they gave each other their hands.

Haidji

Their hands were glued for the third time; but this time, not only with their tears, but also with the blood of their wounds, so nothing could prevent them from being siblings.

They spent the night in the cold, looking at their stars, talking about them, as would they know that nothing or no one could replace them. People are not substitutable; each one has its place in our hearts, places open and close up and new places can come for new people, but no one can take someone else's place, when you really love someone.
They loved those stars, the two children.

The Angel caught them again, hiding, looking there where they shouldn't look, desiring what seemed to be impossible or not to be for them.

The Angel tried to explain to them the reasons, the consequences of their choice, telling them they could go to other families, maybe even different ones; there were thousands of other different stars they could pick to fulfill their life purpose.

Once again, the Angel tried to separate their hands. But they were already siblings. Their blood and tears had bound them together. It wasn't possible to separate them.

They knelt, prayed and begged for it to be, though not noticing that a smile had passed through the Angel's greyish semblance, turning it golden. Because they had shown that they would be able to bear the suffering caused by their, and other persons', decisions in their lives.

The Angel asked them, once again, if they could chose other stars.

As they said no, the Angel asked if they were ready to go through the darkest night, walk over the sharpest ice and bear the deepest indifference to their desires, until their chosen stars could find each other. Things that would thin their bodies, try to damage their souls, and bring them down several times, along the path.

It would be easier, simpler and less painful to chose other stars, be apart and have a more peaceful life.

"NO", answered both children together, "we want these ones and we want to be together".

They would be given the chance to see the stars from above just once more, before leaving and preparing to be delivered into the world of pain.

They sat together, in silence, looking at their stars.

From each star a rose-colored ray of light came to them. Two rays, which they kept between their glued-together hands. Both rays mixed and turned into a heart of rose light, inside their hands.

They stood up and started to walk, hand in hand.

They passed through the coldest nights, were cut by the coldest of the sharpest ice, but nothing was able to damage their souls. They had between their hands the light of their stars, protecting them with the brightness of hope.

Grey sadness dust was present almost all the time, falling over them, trying to make them greyish, falling over their skin and mixing with their tears, then to be dried in the sun and get blown away by the wind.

Even if their feelings and bodies had been hurt, the stars' rays had grown and wrapped around their souls, protecting them. They were beautiful, inside and outside.

One day, without seeking them or being sought by them, their paths would cross with their chosen stars.

Their souls were afraid and scared, but strong, and they gave each other their hands, not trying to escape, not even feeling anxious.

Both stars had met.

The children sighed and looked at each other, their eyes speaking, their souls crying, their eyes smiling.

Perhaps they jumped too much,
Laughed too loud,
Played and disobeyed sometimes.
They were dropping out the dust of pain.

Children, beautiful inside, beautiful outside.
Like their soul parents, rare persons.
Beautiful outside, beautiful inside.

Children.

Haidji

Extremely similar to their parents, as only
soul's children
can be.

Sometimes you meet your children or parents by birth.
Other times your soul children or parents appear in a certain
period of your life.
This doesn't mean they haven't chosen you to be part of their
lives since the beginning.
It only means, they needed to take an unusual path to find
you, or you to find them.

Your parents aren't always your soul parents; your children,
not always your soul children.
Sometimes they are in your life since the beginning,
sometimes only for a moment, sometimes for longer.

But your soul parents or children will be there for you; either
as biological, adopted, step-ones or just someone you
encounter somewhere, when the time is right for it.

To be part of your dreams and life, until it is time for them to go again.

To a place where they are lighter than air, and don't need wings to fly.

Haidji

"Sometimes the best support you can give is your trust and your silence "

Haidji – The Gondola Walker

Haidji

The Gondola Walker

A whisper crossed the air in the middle of the never-ending silence of a Venetian night. It seemed to be the wind, circulating between the apparently sleeping floating gondolas close to San Marco's square.

But even if sometimes the wind plays piano,

moving one gondola after another up and down,

it wasn't the wind,

but a child learning to play the notes of a melody,

walking from one gondola onto the next one,

playing a symphony.

As would each gondola be

a piano key.

While the canals were

the piano strings,

all parts of a mysterious piano,

Playing long after the afternoon is gone.

A piano also called,

The Venetian Lagoon.

Francesco was, after his long day at the gondolier school, sitting on the canal side, watching the gondolas, as he noticed a whisper.

"Can there be a smaller wind inside a bigger wind? A child wind?

Why are the gondolas moving as if they would be playing a song, if there is no wind at all and the current seems quiet? Why are they moving at all?"

With his peripheral vision he saw a blue flowery dress passing close to him and black child-hairs flying like shadows over his gondola.

Francesco was almost half asleep, sitting on the canal side after his long day learning for the last one of his uncountable exams at the gondolier school.

He thought he was dreaming, hearing a whispered Gondolier song, 'Barcarole.'

"I should go home", said Francesco to himself. "It is late and I am daydreaming after the sun already went down."

Allegra, the child, stopped walking around and whispered:
"Ciao Francesco! Ciao Francesco!"

At the moment she saw him standing up, herself running away before he could turn his head far enough to see her, she whispered:

"Go to bed Francesco; sleep well, your final exam is soon. Mine too."

Haidji

Six months, over 400 hours of instruction: Sailing law, English, perfect knowledge of Venice's canals and landmarks. Rigorous examinations testing Francesco's physical endurance, navigational skills, knowledge of Venice's culture and sights.

Francesco was nervous about his final exam to become a Gondolier.

Six months, over 400 hours of learning, while Francesco was learning. Allegra was lucky and happy about Francesco's successes; many Gondola Walkers' Mentors did not come so far.

Nervous about the final exam to become a Gondola Walker, Allegra trained a little bit more inside the Silence of the Venetian night, walking from one Gondola onto a next one, creating melodies inside the silence of a Venetian night.

Learning day after day after day, for months, Francesco couldn't believe he was shortly facing his final exam.

In the past, the ancient profession of being a gondolier used to be passed from father to son. The license, issued by the Municipal Authority, could be handed down from father to son, or a person could become an apprentice as a replacement for an old sonless gondolier, or if no son interested in the job entered the list of suitors. Once an old gondolier died, the municipality would assign his place to the first name on the list. All entries need to pass a qualifying examination, "the proof of the oar" - 'La Prova del Remo". The first period of a replacement's job was hard, serving the suburbs and giving most of the gains to the widow of the old gondolier, for the hire of the gondola.

Nowadays everyone can try to become a gondolier; a person can go to the gondolier school, pass several exams and make an internship with a professional gondolier. After the apprenticeship they have a practical examination in the presence of the 'Five Judges' gondoliers. Not easy. Everyone can try to go to the gondolier school, but only few can pass all the exams, even if the story says that there were between eight to ten thousand Gondolas during the 17th and 18th centuries.

Nowadays there were only about 400 active ones. Everyone can try...

But only few can pass the final exam.

The same gilt for Gondola Walkers: from eight to ten thousand active Gondola walkers in the past, creating magic melodies inside of Venetian nights, they all needed to move away from Venice, as the number of Gondolas would reduce,

because there can only be

as many Gondola Walkers

as there are Gondoliers,

or active Gondolas navigating through the Venetian canals.

A gondola is not just a flat-bottomed Venetian rowing boat.
A gondola is a piece of history and magic.
Magic made using different types of wood,
composed of 280 pieces.
With their left side longer than their right side,
to help to resist the tendency of turning in circles
through Venetian canals,
keeping the magic of ancient times
in every and each moment
since you step inside a gondola
until long after you step out of it,
as would a gondola,
once you stepped inside of it,
get your permission to be
navigating inside your veins
while floating in Venice's canals,
finding a short cut
to bring Venetian soul
directly into your heart.

Francesco was long sleeping as

Haidji

Allegra was still standing on a gondola, seeing San Marco's place for a moment, before taking a step onto a next one on the Venetian Grand Canal.

Allegra smiled, remembering a night, over six months ago.

As she saw the gondoliers trying to stay in equilibrium while she,

tired of walking bridges up and down, or avoiding to walk through the crowd on the streets,

decided for the first time to make her own way,

jumping fast from the top of one gondola onto the next one

...skipping over gondolas

as would they be

the real roofs of a floating city.

The real way to walk through Venice,

thought Allegra,

going from one gondola to a next one, hearing a melody created

by the movement of each gondola she stepped onto.

Venice has 177 canals.

Venetians are usually quiet.

At night, in Venice,

you can recognize persons by their footsteps,

if there are some walking around.

Most individuals are out of view,

So full the city is at daytime, so empty it turns at night.

The streets are not just quiet,

they are completely drowned in silence.

A kind of silence nonexistent in other cities in the world.

In the same magical way colors take your eyes' sight over at daytime, silence takes the city over in a Venetian night.

The Venetian night, when all is dark, quiet and peaceful,

is the time for the Gondola Walkers to arrive.

Arriving for their own and lonely training inside the silence of the night.

Allegra,

jumping from one gondola onto another, saw them arriving.

She couldn't count how many they were,

But they seemed to be over 400, coming from all directions,

walking from gondola to gondola, to meet and play songs together.

A girl saw Allegra and came into her direction.

Haidji

Allegra got scared by seeing so many individuals doing the same as she was trying to do and ran away, all the way from San Marco region to Giardino della Bienalle, over all eight bridges, until she finally arrived in the park, sitting close to Diana's statue.

But, so fast she could run, faster could the other girl run,
a girl called Valentina, was waiting already in front of the statue
as Allegra sat down to rest.
"Who are you?" asked Valentina.
"I...I'm..."
After thinking in silence for a while, she said:
"I'm Allegra!" as would it be the first time she figured her name out. Because she needed to think about it, as would she never have said her name before.
"I'm Valentina. He is Lorenzo", said Valentina, as a boy wearing a dark suit arrived. "I am from the lace island, also called Burano, and Lorenzo is from the Isola di San Michelle...it is..."
Valentina added in a whispered voice... "The cemetery island."

"Do you also live in Venice?" asked Allegra.
"Yes", answered Valentina.
"What were you doing with all those others, jumping over gondolas?"
"We were not jumping, we were walking, playing songs.

We are Venetian Gondola Walkers!" said Valentina, proudly.
"We play songs with the gondolas, so all people can have a good night and La Serenissima can sleep in peace before a new day arrives.

"Who is La Serenissima?" asked Allegra.

"La Serenissima, is the official non-secret sweet nickname of Venice.
Venice is called La Serenissima, La Dominante, Queen of the Adriatic, City of Water, City of Masks, City of Bridges, The Floating City or City of Canals, and probably has other names, more secret, showing other parts of its personality", explained Valentina.

They became friends almost immediately.

Valentina had moved to San Polo, the smaller of the six 'sestieri' (areas) of Venice, close to Rialto Bridge, a couple of years ago coming from Burano, and Lorenzo, Lorenzo escaped from the Isola di San Michele, a former prison island, nowadays Venice's cemetery, to live in "Campo de'l Arsenal" in "Castello", another sestiere of Venice.

Valentina explained she was wearing her white lace dress, because she loved laces and was a lace maker in Burano before becoming a Gondola Walker.

Haidji

Lorenzo never said who he was before moving into Arsenale, but he must have been have an elegant and serious professional, according to his suit, at least that was what Valentina believed it to be, as Lorenzo wasn't much of a speaker.

"Can I become a Gondola Walker too?" asked Allegra.
"What do I need to do?"

"It is not easy, you need to have a Mentor, what means, you need to chose a Mentor and support him for all his learning.
You need to choose someone who wants to become a Gondolier.
Be with him in all hours of his learning, learn all he learns and sometimes help him not to fail, other times jump on the gondola suddenly, so he has an unexpected challenge to deal with.
You can make him better or destroy his career, it is a huge responsibility."

"Once he passes his final exam, you pass yours.
After it, you support him for a few hours a day and have the rest of your time for yourself.
But most important of all, you need to learn how to walk, not to jump from one Gondola onto the next one, to create beautiful balance and notes."

Valentina and Lorenzo, after years of training, were already Gondola Walkers. They used to walk from one Gondola to the next one to create unexpected challenges for the Apprentices after they passed their final exam at the Gondolier school. Still always supporting their mentors, spending every day a few hours with them.

To be a Gondola Walker, they had to find their own way to learn and pass their own exams.

Which they did.

This is how Allegra chose Francesco as her Mentor.

Learning how to equilibrate, walking over his Gondola, as he was learning how to be a Gondolier. Controlling her impulsive nature, walking slow and fast, but not running.

Being so quiet and fast so Francesco could only suspect her presence. Quiet like a Venetian night, she passed all the Exams with him, until the final one came.

Francesco wasn't calm, but he was prepared.

It was the final exam.

He knew how to get the gondola off a sandbar, to back it up, to avoid bumping into canal walls or other gondolas.

Haidji

He knew even how to sing gondoliers' songs.

How to navigate through difficult canals and low bridges, while Allegra walked from one side to the other side of the Gondola,

Lighter than the wind, but confident enough to move it a quarter of a millimeter up or down here or there, equilibrating the gondola.

Trying not to be distracted by tourists, seagulls, or especially by Valentina and Lorenzo,

waiting for her over every bridge they passed under,

trying to support her and Francesco,

whispering indications by the wind,

actually more distracting than helping,

as friends sometimes are,

until Allegra, trying to be focused, screamed...

"Go, wait for me at the end! I will be fine doing it all by myself."

The Gondola almost tipped as she jumped to the end of it, to scream into Valentina's and Lorenzo's direction. What Francesco supposed was a seagull screaming around him, distracting him.

Even before Francesco could react, Allegra walked onto the other end of the Gondola to bring it back into equilibrium and then on the right and left sides, several times, with small steps, reducing the impact until the gondola was floating quietly again.

All this happened so fast, that the judges saw only as would there have been a wind wave, them too, looking for the supposed seagull.

"What happened?" asked Francesco, feeling the wind wave caused by Allegra, as would he be inside a sea wave breaking and calming down at the same time. "I have never seen this before. Is it part of the final exam? Do they throw fast seagulls from the bridges?"

With no time to think about it, or to find the troubled seagull, Francesco continued his exam.

Only one of the judges knew about "The Gondola Walkers", from stories told by his grandfather. A smile crossed his face; the "wave with no water" was for him one of the proofs of their existence.

"Keep going Francesco, you are almost through it. We are almost through it!" whispered Allegra.

"Keep Going Francesco..." Francesco could hear some whisper, as would it be a wind inside of this non-windy day.

Francesco passed his exam and celebrated with his friends.

Allegra celebrated with Valentina and Lorenzo.

When someone is ready and prepared to achieve something, ready and prepared:

Do not try to help.

Just let the person do it by him or her self,

Wait and celebrate together after it.

If you try to help someone who is already ready and prepared,

Sometimes all you achieve is to disturb.

Sometimes the best support you can give is your trust and your silence.

After celebrating with her new friends, Allegra walked into San Marco square, where she was expecting some old friends she wanted to celebrate with.

Allegra decided to go out and walk over gondolas in the daytime, because she was waiting for her visitors to come.

She arrived before them at San Marco's Square, and started walking through the streets of Venice, checking if everything was fine at the hotel they would stay in.

She passed Guilhermo, the fruit seller on one of the bridges, feeling the smell of fruits coming through their colors. "Buongiorno Guilhermo!"

Apart from a few communications, the last time she spoke or saw her friends was months ago, as she moved to Venice, so, she was looking forward to see them again.
There wouldn't be much time to spend time together, but they were coming to visit her.
The last time she saw them, they were kind of sad, scattering ashes over Diana's Statue by moonlight.

Now they were coming to bring her a present, maybe for passing her exam and becoming a Gondola Walker? Even if they did not know about it yet.
All she asked them was to bring her a necklace made of Murano's glass, with flowers. It would be her 'graduation' present.
She was next to them as they chose it in a tourist shop, trying to see if they would chose the right one, but she ran out of the shop quickly before they could see her and she was waiting for them at Giardino as they arrived with her present on the following day.

Haidji

The couple approached Diana's statue and left the present at the statue, for Allegra. Lit a candle for her, dropped some tears, hugged each other and spent some time feeling her presence around them, while their kids were walking around the park.

Allegra saw the necklace hanging on Diana's statue.
A girl walking through the park saw it too and reached for it.
She showed the necklace to her mother, sitting on a nearby bench, asking if she could keep it.
At the moment the mother said 'yes' and put it around the girl's neck,
the same necklace appeared on Allegra's neck
and an image of a man scattering ashes over Diana's statue appeared in front of Allegra's eyes, mind and heart.

For a smaller part of a second, Allegra remembered her son's face, her soul watching her own ashes being scattered, releasing the rest of her and their pain, so she could live as a free and happy girl in Venice.

Allegra kissed a red rose in the garden, saying thanks for the necklace.
The rose fell into a woman's hand and the woman gave her husband the flower.
While Allegra forgot the past once more, and saw the couple as her friends again.

Allegra smiled, dancing around the couple, sending kisses and saying thanks for the new necklace.

As the couple walked away,
Allegra waved goodbye with her new necklace and knew they would think of her, passing in front of the cemetery island, happy about scattering her ashes in the park, on the feet of Diana's statue, where her soul could be free, and she could be found by her destiny.

Until it would be time for her to move on again, and see her friends again somewhere else in the world.

Maybe the best time of her eternal life would be this time between lives,
When freedom, love and friends was all she had and she did not even need air to breathe, when all the air her soul needed to stay alive came through the colors she could see and the songs she could play inside a Venetian night.
Walking around through Venice's streets at daytime, walking over gondolas at night. Being a Gondola Walker.

Haidji

Sometimes the best time in our lives,
is the unexpected time between goals.
The time between all different lives we can have inside of the
same one,
where we are open to magical things to happen.
Suddenly, we see ourselves changing our paths and becoming
something we never dared to be.
Something we never dreamed about before.

Like a Gondola Walker,
playing songs while the night is covering the world,
helping in an invisible way.

Even if we think no one sees us
or realizes the existence of those moments in our lives,
somewhere is someone hearing all the songs we play for the
Earth.

Haidji

"I kissed the ground
because
the sky was too far away"

Haidji – The Wasteland Keeper

Haidji

The Wasteland Keeper

Olivia was not allowed to drink coffee at home.

She was only 8 years old.

But now and then, when she went to play at a neighbor's house,

an old woman, Marlene, gave her a coffee, with two spoons of sugar.

Marlene's house,

wasn't really a house, it was more some pieces of wood nailed together with some metal plates over it.

The garden around the house wasn't a real garden, but a wasteland,

a perfect place for kids to pretend to be in a real jungle,

opening the path to new discoveries;

a nightmare for parents, running to the hospital, searching for stitches or vaccines, as their kids once again got rusted nails in their feet, through their flip-flop sandals or running shoes.

Marlene wasn't a real registered owner,

but she lived there for so many years that she could be recognized as an owner – if she would like to take the place out of the heirs' hands and fight about whether she or the trust fund would pay the taxes for it until it could be decided who owns the place, the Heirs or Her –

living there so many years that even she couldn't remember how many they were. She believes to have been born there.

She lived there for so many years that the whole neighborhood saw it as her place; Marlene became part of the landscape. The ugly part you did not see anymore, focusing only on the beautiful part of your life. Accepting, ignoring and moving on.
A poor house with a big devastated garden,
in the middle of a fancy neighborhood.
Categorized between Wasteland and Magic Space, depending on the point of view or mood of adults or children.

Where people had electronic gates and alarms, and glass shards on top of their walls,
Marlene had an old wall, grey, made by blocks, full of graffiti expressions and drawings.
Where people had house walls, she had wood plates.
Where people had swimming pools, she had an old tub, covered with cement to fill the holes.
Where they had slides and swings, she had old tires and mounds of earth.
Where people had a ceiling, she had metal plates,
of the kind that seemed to be singing as raindrops fell over them.

A paradise for kids,

a nightmare for real estate agents trying to sell the houses around her place, as some were free and available from time to time.

A cup of coffee with 2 spoons of sugar is what she offered to all her visitors, kids or adults.

For the kids, she was the keeper of a magical place.

For adults, the wasteland keeper.

No matter what point of view, she was the keeper as each and every one of them enjoyed her coffee.

Now and then Olivia was allowed to visit Marlene and spend some time in paradise. A place where she could take her sandals, flip-flops or running shoes off, leave them on the ground and climb a tree.

Walking around the Coffee trees, also called Coffea trees, from time to time she tasted some of the red or purple fruits, chewing the seeds, the two coffee beans she could find inside of it, laughing as Marlene told her not to eat raw coffee beans, better to search for berries, bananas or other edible raw things.

"Coffee you need to prepare yourself and make the coffee so you can drink it, it is not a banana or a berry, Olivia, which you can take directly from nature and eat. Coffee has deeper secrets and needs preparation from both sides and from time." Bringing her a cup of coffee, as Olivia used to come down from the trees.

All that Marlene had to offer to Olivia was paradise and a cup of coffee.

Marlene had a face as would she already have been born old. Hairs as would they always have been grey.
So far as Olivia could remember, she was old, grey and magical.
Olivia couldn't remember her in a different way. She was old since Olivia saw her the first time; probably she had never been younger, thought Olivia from time to time. There was a rumor between the kids, saying that Marlene was a tree spirit, turned into a human to protect the trees in this garden, so kids could have a real place to play.

Marlene thought she had only coffee to offer, while she offered all the neighbor kids a piece of paradise.

Some people give more than they think they do, or can, because they do not really know how much they really have, or the value of what they are giving.

Olivia spent most time of her childhood's free time in this place where trees were stairs to heaven.
A place far away from all the noise of her daily life, school and TV; a place where kids could create their own adventures.

As Olivia turned 13, Olivia's family moved away and took Olivia with them, despite her wish to stay there. She finished growing up in an apartment condominium on the other side of town, with the beauty of her childhood memories: Marlene, the magic place, and the cup of coffee...

As Olivia turned 18 and got her own car and with it a piece of freedom, she decided to visit the magic place. Olivia was sad about her older brother living abroad since a few years ago, and mostly about herself, moving out soon, with an uncertain faith, going to university. Would she be able to achieve her goals? Fulfill her own dreams? Sometimes she felt so alone with her decisions.

Even if it was what she decided to do, she was sad about moving away from her parents' house. Unsure about being able to do it, not sure if she could be happy moving again into a new place. Searching for a physical proof of paradise, she parked her car in a nearby street and walked slowly in the direction of Marlene's house, afraid to see if Marlene would still live there, or even remember her. Should she turn back?

Olivia forced herself to keep walking, in slow motion, as would she be a child again, expecting the Earth to turn backwards to her steps' direction, making her steps be slow jumps, as would the Earth itself be carrying her into the place she was trying to go.

Whether it was the Earth's rotation or her own feet moving, Olivia arrived.

Marlene was still living in the same house.

There were holes on the walkway in front of her place. Weeds growing out of those holes. Broken wall pieces around, over and who knows, maybe even under those weeds.

"Are my memories faked? Did my sense of beauty change? This place is so miserable", mumbled Olivia to herself, as she saw the old broken wall from the street, trash on the sidewalk, and weeds all over the place.

"Poor Marlene, living in a wood house, no real roof over her head and weeds all around her house, this all looks so devastated.

I shouldn't come back here and destroy my memories."

If you go back to places you were as a child,

people you met in the past,

see people you admired as a child;

There is a risk for you to devastate your memories and crush your feelings.

Places are mostly not so big or beautiful as you remember them to be, people not so

intelligent,

as you supposed them to be.

Situations are not exactly as you remember them to be;

time paints your memories with different colors.

Drawn into the moment, into the feeling you had in this moment, you could see only part of reality, this part is intensified and grows with time passing by, erasing all other aspects of your memories.

Maybe paradise has been inside a cup of coffee.

Living in other places, Olivia was able to come back and see the place through different eyes.

She wasn't blind-happy anymore, the kind that ignores the trash and sees only the beauty around. Being depressed, all she saw was the trash.

Olivia decided to enter the place, trying to watch her own steps, not to fall walking with high heels over all the holes, weeds and stones on the path, as an old woman came in her direction.

"Good Morning, can I help you?"

All that Olivia could say was:

"Marlene?"

then she closed and opened her eyes three or four times and added:

"Marlene, are you still living here, after all these years?

I'm Olivia, do you remember me?"

Unconsciously she took her shoes off, speaking to Marlene, in veneration to the place or to her shoes, maybe a mix of both.

Respecting the place, taking care of her shoes, feeling the taste of the Earth with bare feet.

"Olivia, oh yes! Olivia!

Kids grow up so fast, you are a woman now!

Do you still like coffee?"

"Marlene, how can you live here? Aren't you sad? Do you need something?" Not answering about the coffee offer.

Marlene didn't answer either.

All Marlene did was to smile,

and invited Olivia to enter her 'house'.

Olivia followed her.

In silence Marlene made her a cup of coffee, boiling the water in an old wood burning stove, using coffee beans out of her own garden's trees, burned and ground by herself, passing the coffee through an old cloth coffee strainer into an old coffee pot.

Olivia never watched Marlene preparing the coffee before. She was speechless; as a child she was more focused on the garden, with no idea about the ritual it could be, the creation of a simple cup of coffee.

Marlene poured the coffee in an old metal cup, took a small silver spoon from a glass containing different cutlery pieces, opened an old can whose image faded away a long time ago; taking sugar out of it, pausing the spoon a few centimeters over the cup, letting the sugar slide into it, as the sun, coming through the door, reflecting on the sugar crystals, made it seem like a river of diamonds, flowing into the darkness of the coffee.

Marlene then dropped the spoon into the coffee and mixed it slowly in a clockwise direction, whispering:

"May coffee and sugar mix as would they be day and night and bring joy and happiness into all moments of life."

Marlene offered the coffee cup to a speechless Olivia.

Olivia drank her cup of coffee from the old, dented metal cup.

The taste of the coffee brought her memories back, intensifying them again.

Olivia could see the beauty again, even if she did not ignore the poverty of the place, because, to see beauty and be happy does not consist in ignoring the bad things, focusing only on the good side of life.

But in acknowledging the bad, and seeing the beauty, in spite of it.

In being able to be happy, even with problems, and trash in your life.

Being able to live one moment at a time, preparing yourself for the battles and happiness of the next one.

Marlene's words were still echoing in her mind: "...day and night..."

Sometimes all you need is the right cup of coffee, to see the beauty in front of you. Olivia felt as would she be on the top of a tree, surrounded by the blue of the sky, happy and confident about achieving her goals and dreams.

Olivia went out of the house, went down on her knees and kissed the ground in front of Marlene's door.

Marlene asked:
"Olivia, what are you doing?"

Olivia answered:
"I kissed the ground because
the sky was too far away.

As my lips touched the ground
an overwhelming feeling took over.
I felt love for the Earth, which made me rise,
so I could touch the sky.

Then I realized I love the place I'm in
as much as I used to love the sky,
climbing this garden's trees, feeling so close to it."

Marlene smiled.

Olivia said good-bye to Marlene, not sure if she would ever
see her again.
Her University was abroad.
A new step in her life would begin.

One of the first things Olivia bought for her new place was a
coffee maker.
It wasn't old, but new, it was an Italian moka pot.
Which she used to make coffee for herself and for her
colleagues or friends, when they came to visit her.

Whispering in her thoughts:

"May coffee and sugar mix as would they be day and night, and bring joy and happiness into all moments of life."

Sometimes she cried, remembering Marlene, wondering how she was doing or if she was still alive. Sometimes she smiled remembering the beautiful moments in paradise.
Paradise and wasteland, together in one single place,
inside and outside Olivia's heart, life and mind.
Olivia learned to be happy, despite all the trash in her life.
Not ignoring it, but seeing that no matter how hard life can be sometimes,
everyday there are beautiful things, big things, small things, like a cup of coffee.
Coffee that isn't only a dark powder mixed with hot water, but the seeds of a fruit, life seeds from a tree, grown under the sunlight.
Roasted by fire, ground, filtering the water of life, for you to drink, fully filled with secrets inside, revealed only after preparation from both sides, the coffee and the person drinking it, bringing happiness into day and night.

Because sometimes, paradise can be there, close to you, every morning, inside your cup of coffee, bringing joy and happiness into your daily life; helping you to wake up, so you can see all different aspects of your life.

Haidji

Haidji

"When no one and nothing can remind me
that free will stops
when you have conscience of all"

Haidji – Would you love...an Angel?

Haidji

Would you love...an Angel?

Would you love...an Angel?
Make me smile while I cry
and feel...I'm yours...tonight.

Seeing my real face in front of you
while you're dancing by wind sounds.
Without bringing me memories of someone else,
or making me see another face covering yours.
Just being yourself...without masks or illusions,
because a mask, a mask falls short before the first tear comes.

Would you love...an Angel?
Make me cry while I smile
and feel...I'm here...tonight.

Hearing the music of your skin touching mine,
while I'm sliding through your fingers.
Singing the words we speak between kisses.
So I can stop to be who I am for a while,
to be, just yours tonight.
When no one and nothing can remind me that free will
stops when you have conscience of all.

Would you love...an Angel?
Make me smile while I cry

and be...so much...tonight.

You cannot stop the pain if you don't know the fountain.
You cannot use a sword without to touch it,
feel a dream you never had, or be inside a world you don't believe in.
Without faith, even if I would cry tears of pure...blood
or almost not touch the ground while I walk,
Earth's magma would burn my feet and I would need to fly,
to fly away,
if you would try, with no faith.

Would you love...an Angel?
Make me cry while I smile
and be...just...yours...tonight.

Even if I don't belong to this world and to no one else,
I cannot replace someone else inside your heart.
Someone's destiny can bring tomorrow, or maybe not.
Maybe there is a place for me after all.
So, I came to you with only one question beyond all my words,
while you were
eating knowledge fruits from my mouth, swallowing them,
drinking wisdom.

Would you love...an Angel?
Make me smile while I cry
and paint on me...tonight.

Haidji

Let me kiss you with petals of roses,
seeing their blood over your skin.
As would it be me, crying over you.
Between you and me
the pain of pleasure, passion...love.
Loosing myself...inside of you,
feeling you inside of me.
Without rules, limits...being able to stop the time...for you.

Would you love...an Angel?
Make me cry while I smile.
Paint inside of me...tonight.

Killing all worlds we know to create a new one.
Beyond all pain, pleasure, passion.
Too strong to stop, too weak to say no.

When the mind sleeps, the heart beats and the soul speaks.
Blood turns into magma inside our veins,
exploding like colored stars.

Would you love...an Angel?
Make me smile while I cry
and feel...I'm here...tonight.

Ask me to believe in things I can't.
Make me dream impossible moments.
When life is so beautiful like only a dream can be.

I came to you with all this silence beyond my words,
as all I wanted to know
was the answer to a simple question:

Would you love...an Angel?
Make me cry while I smile
and feel you...tonight.

Haidji

"Some stars are twins
Some stars are brothers
Some stars are...lovers
· These are the most rare ones"

Haidji – Stars

Haidji

Stars

Some stars are twins
Some stars are brothers
Some stars are... lovers
- These are the most rare ones

Stars are born as twins somewhere in the universe.
The lover type, breaks their bodies or souls before they meet
each other.
Which allows them to become one... one day.

Some stars are twins
Some stars are brothers
Some stars are... lovers
- These are the most rare ones

Stars grow up breaking their parts,
Feeling the pain, surviving the sorrow.
For every tear they cry,
Sparks of their light illuminate the path
Of life where they will meet each other.

Some stars are twins

Some stars are brothers

Some stars are... lovers

- These are the most rare ones.

Haidji

About the Author

Writer, artist, painter, designer, photographer, performer. Just...**Haidji**.

Her interest in art began at the age of four when she got a blackboard for Christmas. She then started to draw objects around the house: chairs, tables, and so on. As she was twelve, she started to write her stories and poems. Handwritten and hand-painted books, for family and friends.

Her University education was at the University of Applied Science at Idar-Oberstein, Germany, where she obtained a Master's Degree in Jewelry and Precious Stones Design, and Painting. She is also a qualified and awarding-winning Goldsmith.

Haidji is a talented and creative artist who produces abstract work that resonates with warmth and life.

Her stories create images in the reader's mind, as would a word be a brushstroke painting inside your imagination.

There is a very spiritual feel to her work, almost an otherworldliness. A captiving blend of Brazilian flair, Teutonic precision and Dutch pragmatism makes Haidji's work unique, appealing and thought-provoking.

Since 1995 Haidji has exhibited her work, realised her projects and told her stories in many countries: Germany, Brazil, Italy, The Netherlands, Switzerland, England, Portugal, Spain, South Africa, Australia, Canada and the United States of America.

A personal note from Haidji, for her readers:

Thank you very much for reading my book.
If you enjoyed this book, please consider leaving an online review; even if it's only a line or two, it would make all the difference, and would be very much appreciated.

Best wishes,
Haidji

Contacts:

Blog – **www.haidji.blogspot.com**
Email – **haidji@gmail.com**
Facebook official page – Haidji
Twitter – @Haidji
Instagram · @haidjiofficialprofile

Haidji